# JOEL
## IN
# TANANAR

ROBERT M. WALTON

Padre Productions   1982   San Luis Obispo

Printed in the United States of America

Illustrated by Jon Dahlstrom
Cover design by Lachlan P. MacDonald
and Michelle Hires

Published by Padre Productions, P.O. Box 1275
San Luis Obispo CA 93406

# Dedication

To Pat Bratton and John White. You've both helped me tame recalcitrant commas—and considerably more. Your friendship has certainly made possible the writing of this book. Thanks—and thanks again.

The Road goes ever on and on
    Down from the door where it began.
Now far ahead the Road has gone,
    And I must follow, if I can.

Pursuing it with weary feet.
    Until it joins some larger way,
Where many paths and errands meet.
    And whither then?  I cannot say.


by

J. R. R. Tolkien

# JOEL IN TANANAR

## Table of Contents

*Against the old man's brown palm*
*lay what looked like a small sun.*

# I

## Joel's Tree

Joel Burnham looked at the scratch on Mr. Gravit's desk. It was a curling scratch that cut deeply into the shiny wood. He was getting to know that scratch pretty well.

"Joel, this is the fourth time in less than a month that you've been sent to see me." Mr. Gravit tapped his pencil against the desk as he waited for an answer.

Joel shifted from one foot to the other and said, "Yes."

"Well?"

Joel looked up quickly. Mr. Gravit was a heavy man with a pink, bald head. He had cranked his face into its worst expression. "Well?" When he frowned, the wrinkles piled up so high on his forehead that they finally fell down the back of his neck. Joel decided it was time to say something.

"He called me a pig."

Somehow, this sounded much sillier, much more childish than Joel had thought it would. Mr. Gravit looked like Joel had just pinched him.

"Oh, now I see. Now I see!" It was plain to Joel that Mr. Gravit didn't see. "Because Bobby Twist called you a name you hit him on the nose. Then, not to be outdone, he hit you on the nose right back. In the process of trading nose blows you knocked a desk over on Miss Gomp's foot causing her to spill the fish tank. It was only through the quick action of two of your classmates that the fish were saved. How Miss Gomp's foot is I cannot say. She is at the hospital right now. All of this happened because Bobby called you a silly name!"

Mr. Gravit stopped for breath. His face was now the color of a radish. Joel looked at the floor. His head was hurting. Bobby hadn't won the fight, but he'd done a

9

good job of losing it. Mr. Gravit was waiting for him to speak. There was nothing he could say. He held back his tears.

"Joel," the voice was softer, "ever since I've been principal of this school I've never met anyone like you. I've tried to be fair, but you are always in trouble. You do only the work which pleases you and you ignore the rest. And you fight. You fight with everyone in your class. You seem to fight for the fun of it. Do you enjoy hurting people?"

Joel felt the sting in the question. The silence which followed was long and full of meaning.

Finally, Mr. Gravit said, "This behavior has got to stop! I'm afraid that you are going to have to stay out of school for awhile. I'm going to notify your mother that your case will have to go before the school board. I know your mother understands my position. We may allow you to return to school at the beginning of next term—if you decide to behave better."

Mr. Gravit waited for a moment, "Does that sound fair?"

It didn't, but Joel nodded yes. He listened numbly as Mr. Gravit went on, "It's not fun to be alone all day. I don't think that you will enjoy being separated from the other children. It should give you something to think about. I hope you do!"

He looked at Joel again.

"That's all. You may go home now." He pulled a drawer open and started looking for an important piece of paper. Joel blinked hard. Tears were coming. He wouldn't cry in front of the principal. He turned and walked out. As the door to the office shut, Mr. Gravit was still searching through the drawer.

Bright, cold afternoon surrounded Joel as he walked out of the school building. An October wind blew yellow light and large, golden sycamore leaves across the wide front lawn. He wiped his tears away and watched the leaves go by. They looked like stars rolling point over end. He jumped down the steps and tried to catch one, but it went bouncing by him. He felt sad when it lifted into the air and went sailing across the playground. Slowly he began walking through the grass.

The way home was not long, but he stopped when he reached the old country road. He stood thinking for a moment. It couldn't be later than four-thirty, and there wasn't much to do at home anyay. Also, his mother would not be happy about what had happened at school. He made up his mind and turned down the road. His secret hide-out lay in an orchard a half-mile out of town. It wasn't much, just a hollowed out place between the roots of an apple tree, but he had $3.95 and some candy buried in a tin box there.

He reached his tree and hopped down into the hollow. It gave him some shelter from the wind. Quickly he dug up the tin box and checked its contents. Everything was still there. He carefully put it on the top of a large root, opened it, and removed a chocolate bar, unwrapped it, and took a bite.

He chewed and thought. He was glad he had never shown Bobby Twist where his box was hidden. Bobby probably would have run out here after their fight and stolen the money. They had once been friends. They had had fun together. Last summer they had spent a whole day hiding from Jill Timber and her eighth grade friends. Joel laughed as he thought of what had happened.

The girls were standing by the dime store trying to impress some high school guys. As if they ever could! Jill was about to spring the braces on her teeth smiling at them. Then the first water balloon hit her, BLURP, right on top of the head. She croaked like a frog and began jumping up and down. That really impressed the high school guys! He and Bobby ran to the orchard while Jill and her friends searched the town for them. Joel smiled. He hated them all now. Joel chewed harder on his candy bar.

Suddenly, he heard the clear, low notes of a bird's song. He looked up and saw a small, yellow bird. It was sitting on a branch right above his head. He had never seen such a bird. Its feathers shone softly in the sunlight. Its eyes were deep, shining black. It sang brightly for several minutes. Joel sat staring for a moment when the song ended. The bird fluttered to a lower branch. It settled itself, cocked its head and looked into Joel's eyes.

A strange feeling now came over him. He knew that he wasn't the best student in school, but he had learned enough to know that people aren't supposed to talk to birds. Still, he felt that the bird expected him to say something. He felt he should say hello. But he picked up a rock instead. He took careful aim and . . . he couldn't move his arm. The bird threw back its head and trilled a series of notes that sounded like laughter. Then, looking once more at Joel, it flashed into the sky and vanished.

"There, that's better!" said a voice behind him.

Joel turned around so fast that he knocked over his tin box. All of the money and candy spilled out on the ground. One quarter rolled down the root, wobbled over dusty leaves, and bumped into an even more dusty boot. Joel looked at the boot and its companion. Slowly he let his eyes rise up to the face of the owner. It was an old face. It had a long, sharp nose and at least ten thousand wrinkles.

"Are you Joel?" The voice was dry-sounding.

Joel's voice shook a little as he said, "Yes, I am. Who are you?"

"I'm just an old man. Old men don't really need names." A wide smile crinkled the brown face even more. He seemed to be harmless even though his clothes

12

were very ragged. Joel decided that he wasn't afraid of the old man, at least not very much.

He said, "What do you mean by that? Why don't old men need names?"

"Well," said the man, "only young men like you need names. You have a list of things that you've done, things that you are. At the very top of that list is your name. Your name stands for you. It sums up your history. Very old men can't use names. Their lists are too long. They've done far too much. Their names no longer fit them."

Joel was puzzled. He said, "I don't understand what you're talking about. Old men have names."

The man said, "What's your grandfather's name?"

Joel said, "It's Grandfather."

"No," said the man, "What was his name when he was your age?"

Joel said nothing.

The man said, "See what I mean? His name doesn't fit him anymore. He doesn't use it."

Joel was beginning to feel angry with this strange man. "Well, what was your name?"

For a moment the old man looked sad and then he spoke, "I would like one simple name, but none will fit me. I've been too many places and done too many things. Any that I choose would be wrong."

Joel said, "You must be called something. You just can't wander around without a name."

The old man smiled, "Call me Telmeer. Yes, Telmeer. Telmeer actually means grandfather in one of the languages which I speak. I'm not really a grandfather, but I'm old enough to be one."

Joel was uncomfortable in the silence that settled over them. It was getting late. The old man watched him expectantly. Joel was figuring something out. He said, "Telmeer?"

13

"Yes?"

"You know my name. You must have come looking for me. You want something from me. What is it?"

Telmeer laughed quietly to himself and then said, "I have been waiting for you to ask me that!" He paused for a moment. "I came to offer you a deal."

Joel said, "What kind of a deal?"

Telmeer said, "I'm not going to tell you that just yet. Let me tell you first why I'm offering this deal to you. It's very simple. You are in trouble and can't get out of it by yourself."

Joel was angry now, "What are you talking about? I can take care of myself! You don't know anything about me."

Telmeer said, "Joel, Joel, I'm just telling you the truth. I'm just telling you what you already know. You're in trouble. Is there any person in this town who likes you? Grown-ups don't like you. Other children don't like you. Your name stands for nothing but a list of bad things. Isn't that true?"

Joel said nothing and didn't move.

"Well, whether you say so, or not, I think that what I have said is pretty much right. There is great anger within you, Joel. It is red and hot. Anyone who comes close to you receives a gift of flames. You never keep friends. Those who want to like you—teachers or children—cannot find you through your anger. You don't know what it is like to have a friend. You don't know how to be a friend."

Joel turned his head and looked toward the setting sun.

Telmeer said, "Your father died." He paused.

Joel looked down at the brown leaves beneath his feet.

Telmeer went on, "Your father died four years ago. His death hurt you greatly. Your wound has never healed. Healing—understanding—never came for you as it did for your mother. Your pain is greater now than it was at first. You hold it close. Pain without healing becomes anger. Always. True?"

14

Joel still said nothing.

Telmeer smiled to himself, "True. Anyway, you need a change, a real change. You need to be able to get outside of yourself. You need to get away from your own troubles. You are young enough to be healed of your hurt, young enough to add many good things to that list of yours. You just need a chance. But people here have already decided that you are bad and always will be bad. Are you strong enough to change their opinions by yourself? You could use some help."

Joel lost his temper. He jumped up and shouted, "I don't want your help. I'm fine the way I am! I don't care what they think about me. I hate them! I hate them!"

He started to run from the tree and the old man, but something held him back. Telmeer looked down and was silent. Slowly Joel sat down again. After several moments Telmeer spoke.

His voice was calm, "Joel, you are the only person who knows all of the things which are on your list. The most important thing about your name is what it means to you. Are you proud of Joel Burnham? Do you like Joel Burnham? No, don't answer me. Just think. Just think. I can't make you do anything. I can only offer you my deal. Will you listen to me?"

Joel was angry, but he was also curious. He muttered, "Go ahead."

Telmeer said, "I will offer you a gift. It is very valuable. If you take it, you must do a job for me."

Joel was now unbearably curious. He said, "What is this gift, anyway?"

Telmeer put his hand deep into his ragged coat and pulled something out. He opened his hand.

Joel gasped. Against the old man's brown palm lay what looked like a small sun. Its brightness was blinding. Slowly the silver light dimmed and he could see an egg-shaped jewel. For the second time that afternoon Joel felt extremely strange. The jewel was pale, clear yellow, except for the center where a burning, white spark floated. Without thinking he reached out and took the jewel from Telmeer's hand. It was cool and smooth. It felt...right. He held it with both hands and said, "This will be mine?"

Telmeer said, "Yes. It has come to you across the darkness between worlds. If you take it, you will be its guardian."

Joel said, "What? What do you mean?"

Telmeer said, "It would have burned you if you were not meant to hold it. Let me tell you a story."

Joel said, "A story?"

"Yes," said the old man, "it will explain things a little. It will help you to understand what lies ahead. Listen."

"There is a land called Tananar. Long ago a great, black fish swam in close to this land, by a city called Marl. The fish swam weakly and finally it stopped. All of the people of the city came to watch the fish. None dared go near. Plainly, the fish was dying. Only one small girl was not afraid. She walked down the shore and into the shallow waters.

"She came to the head of the fish and reached out to touch it. It was hot from the sun and dry. Quickly she cupped her hands and brought up cold water to pour over the dull scales. The fish moved. It spoke, 'You are kind, child, but I am dying.'

"The girl backed away. The fish spoke again, 'Stand before me. It is hard for me to see now.' The girl was frightened, but she moved until she stood in front of one, large eye. 'There,' said the fish, 'I can see you.'

"Its voice was gentle. The girl lost her fear. It said, 'I have carried a burden over the sea. It is time now that I pass it on. I must find out if you are one who is able to carry it. Step closer.'

"The girl did so. She looked into the soft, green depths of the fish's eye. She felt the wonder and the mystery of the deep ocean's unending quiet. She felt the joy of swimming free . . . She stepped back and turned to hide the beginnings of her tears. The fish was dying. She could do nothing to help.

"It said, 'Child you are able. Take this jewel called Lor. It is a charm of great power, of magic. It can be used for good, or for evil. Use it always for good. And guard it. Guard it well.' As the sound of the words faded, the fish's life followed them into silence. It was dead.

"The girl cried and her tears mixed with the waters of the incoming tide. After a time, she looked up and saw the jewel hanging from a silver chain around the fish's neck. The setting sun had surely left a spark behind, an ember of noon. She took hold of it and found it cool to her touch. She tugged it lightly and the chain parted. Slowly she walked back up the sands. She held Lor before her. When the people of the city saw her, they parted and let her pass.

"All of her life she used Lor well. In her hands its great power cured many ills, defeated many evils. And before she died she passed it on . . ."

Telmeer folded his hands and was quiet.

Joel said, "What does your story have to do with me? You still haven't told me what I am supposed to do."

Telmeer sighed. "Joel, the jewel you hold is Lor. Only the jewel's guardian can safely use its power. If you choose to become the guardian of Lor, you also choose to become the user of its power. Much work awaits the guardian. This is my deal. I offer you a treasure and ask labor from you in return. Take the jewel. Use it to help others. You may find that you have helped yourself as well."

Joel said, "I don't understand. Why am I the one? How did I get chosen?"

Telmeer looked straight into Joel's eyes, "I don't know. Lor's power is a mystery. The jewel carried me here to you. Always before it has found a child from its own world. I even thought I knew who would receive it. I was wrong."

17

Joel said, "Then . . . how can you know so much about me."

Telmeer smiled, "I did not present Lor to you immediately. I waited. I watched. I made sure that nothing had interfered with the proper working of the magic. I found out a great deal. I chose this time to explain to you — as much as I myself understand. Now," he paused, "Lor has found you. Will you take it and the work which goes with it?"

Joel began to feel stubborn. He said, "Maybe. I might take it. I want to think. I still don't know enough. I'm not sure that I want to work for you."

Telmeer held out his hand. He said, "There is nothing to think about. Give me back the jewel, or keep it for as long as you live. Choose now."

Joel stood up. He looked at the jewel in his hand. He looked at Telmeer. Quickly he put Lor in his pocket and stepped back three steps. He said, "I'm going to think about it. You can't make me do anything. You're just a ragged old man!"

Telmeer smiled and lowered his hand. He said, "Know this, Joel Burnham. Take the jewel from this place and it is yours. You will be called to Tananar. There, you will find the work you must do. Your choice is here, now."

Joel said, "I'm not choosing anything! I'll talk to you tomorrow. I'll let you know tomorrow."

Telmeer said nothing. He only smiled.

Joel said, "I'm going home now, good-bye." He turned and walked a few steps. Nobody could decide for him. He turned around to say so, but Telmeer was gone. The old man had disappeared. Joel ran back to look into his hollow. No one was there. He shivered. He put his hand in his pocket. Lor was still there. He hadn't been dreaming. He felt confused and he felt scared. Quickly he turned and began to run down the old country road. He didn't stop running until he got to the porch of his house. He rushed inside and slammed his own back door behind him.

# II

## To Tananar

Joel watched leafless elm branches move in the wind. Now and then one scratched against his window. They looked like a bat's wings and claws. He pulled the covers up tighter around his head.

The door to his room opened. Joel raised his eyes. His mother stood in the doorway with her hand still on the knob. She hesitated for a moment and then walked over to his bed. She sat down. Her face was framed by yellow light streaming in from the hall. She said, "Joel?"

He didn't move.

"Joel, I know you're awake. Please listen to me. I . . . I was very angry with you when you came home this afternoon. Mr. Gravit called me. He told me—well, you know what he told me. I lost my temper with you. You've done wrong, but I shouldn't have gotten so angry." She put her hand on his head, tussled his hair. "I've fixed you something to eat. Come into the kitchen and sit with me for awhile."

Joel said nothing and did not move. His mother removed her hand and sat in the semidarkness looking down at him. He could not see the tears in her eyes, but he knew that they were there. Finally, she rose and walked back through the doorway. She turned and looked at him once again and then shut the door softly behind her.

A hot, hard lump had somehow formed in his throat. He tried to swallow it and couldn't. He took Lor from beneath his pillow to place on the table beside his bed. It glowed faintly in his hand, warm to his touch. This should have surprised him, but he hardly noticed it. He looked deep into the jewel and saw—

He saw golden afternoon light spilling over a green and endless sea. He felt himself being drawn to this sea, pulled by this sea. He tried to look away and couldn't. Suddenly, the low, soft sound of large waves was around him. A salt breeze plucked at his hair. He was floating above surging water. In the near distance he could see a shore and the shining towers of a city. He closed his eyes. This could not be. This just could not be.

Joel kept his eyes closed for a time, a very confusing and frightening time. At last, he felt a thump and knew that he was no longer floating through the air. He smelled wood smoke. He heard the crackling of flames and felt the sharp cold of an autumn wind. His eyes opened just a tiny crack and he found himself looking across a campfire at the biggest, ugliest man he had ever seen. The only reason he didn't scream out loud was that the man spoke before his tongue could move.

"Now, Joel, I know what you're thinking. Don't be afraid, though, until I've told you who I am. I'm your friend even if you don't believe me just yet. I have a tale to tell you. Will you give me a chance to tell it?"

Joel sat up and shivered. The man was huge. He was over seven feet tall and his arms were long and thick. His face was all lumpy and knobby. His eyes were small, but they glittered brightly in the firelight. His skin seemed to be a nut-brown color. Joel looked for the best way to run. It was then that he saw a large axe laying by the fire. He decided to stay very still instead. He shivered again, his thin pajamas no protection against the night cold.

"Here," the giant said gruffly, "put these on."

Strangely the clothes he handed Joel—linen shirt, leather pants and cloak of wool— seemed made just for him.

The man spoke again, "Will you give me a listen?"

Joel, still speechless, nodded. The big man's rumbling voice sounded like a landslide as he began his tale. "You are now in Tananar. At least, you are near Tananar. How you got here I can't begin to tell you. It has something to do with Lor."

20

Joel held the jewel more tightly in his hand. The big man smiled knowingly and went on. "Yes, I know you have Lor. That is why you are here. But more of that later. First, I must explain myself. I bet I gave you quite a scare when you woke up."

Joel trembled and stammered "Ye— yes."

The big man laughed loudly, "Well, it couldn't be helped. A long time ago I was somewhat smaller and somewhat prettier than I am now. In fact, I was a normal man. I made my living as a blacksmith. True, I lacked some other qualities. I ate and drank a bit too much and I was never known for being kind. I also liked a good fight now and then. But I enjoyed my life. I enjoyed it until the day that the Witch Queen came to my smithy.

"Of course, I didn't know then that she was the Witch Queen, I thought that she was just some old woman come to have her frying pan fixed. Ah, I was wrong. She came hobbling up grinning with her one yellow tooth and asked me to make a door handle for her. I thought that that was a strange request. She dulled my curiosity, though, by putting five gold pieces in my hand. And she said that she would give me fifty more when I completed the door handle. Fifty! I said I'd take the job. Then she laughed and reached in the big bag she carried at her side. She pulled out a yellow piece of paper. On it was a drawing of an evil-looking snake. She told me to make a mold that looked like that snake. Usually, I would have turned down something like that. However, fifty gold pieces is nothing to sneeze at!

"It took me over a week to finish the mold. During that time I did nothing else. My regular customers complained, but I ignored them. Exactly an hour after I finished the mold, the old woman came to my forge. She said that she had brought the metal to make the door handle. I told her that the mold was finished. I was very proud of it. That snake was the best piece of work that I've ever done. She looked at it and said that it would do. Then, she reached into that bag of hers and pulled out a bar of silver. It was the purest, whitest, silver I've ever seen. She handed it to me and told me to use it for the door handle.

"Well, I stoked up the fire and got to work. That silver was strange stuff. It seemed almost alive when I got it melted down. It twisted and coiled all over the bottom of my melting pot. I ladled it into the mold and waited a bit. Then, so, so carefully, I opened the mold. Perfect! I got out my tools. Slowly, with chisel and boiling acid, I sketched in its features. My hand has never been steadier, let me tell you! Finally, I brought the finished handle out of the cooling tank for the last time. It was evil, but beautiful, too—a silver-white, shining snake. The old woman sighed and reached out her hand to take it from me. I fairly jumped out of my skin! The handle moved between my fingers just as if it were a live snake. I let it drop. She caught it, though, before it touched the floor and laughed softly while I shook in fright. She turned to go.

"Well, I've never thought of myself as a coward, but it was all I could do to say what I said next. I asked her for my fifty gold pieces. She turned her head and looked at me with cold eyes. I almost froze I was so frightened, but I'm stubborn, too. I told her again that she owed me fifty pieces of gold.

"She began to laugh. It was a low, nasty sound at first, but it got louder. Her laughing got so loud that the rafters began to shake and the fire went out. I just stood there. Then, she put her hand deep down in her bag. She grinned as she pulled it out. In her hand she held a purple bottle. Looking at me all the while she reached up and pulled out the cork. She raised the bottle above her head and threw the contents at me. I covered my eyes against the purple liquid. When it touched me, I seemed to catch on fire. I burned. The pain of the burning was so great that I couldn't even cry out. I fell to the floor and lay there until the next morning.

"When I came to my senses, sunshine was falling through my window. The Witch Queen was gone. The memory of pain was bright in my mind, though. I got to my feet and banged my head on the roof. It was then that I knew that something was wrong. I stumbled to the door and had to duck my head to get out. I went out into the street. A girl was carrying a duck to the market. She saw me, threw down her duck, and ran away. It was that way all over the village. Every person who saw me ran screaming into his house to lock his door.

"As you can guess, the Witch had changed me into the big, ugly creature that I am now. Do you think that I look pretty bad?" Joel nodded. "In your world you have stories about trolls, don't you?" Joel nodded and tried to move back slowly.

"Well, they are just rumors. Here in Tananar we have the real thing—terribly strong brutes who look just like me. They roam the hills at night and try to find humans to eat."

Joel swallowed dryly.

"No, no, don't worry. I'm not a real troll. I just look like one. That's my problem."

He was silent for a moment. Then he went on, "To make a long story short, everyone was scared to death of me. Even after they found out that I wasn't a real troll. Real trolls are killed by sunshine, you know; they turn to stone when it touches them. Well, the people couldn't get used to having me around. No one would come to my smithy. Finally, I gave up trying to be a blacksmith and moved out into the forest. No one sees me out here, and here I've lived for many years. Now and again I see the king's soldiers. You see, I earn my bread by helping to protect the borders of Tananar. West of here lie evil lands.

Trolls and talking wolves sometimes come through the woods to raid peaceful folk. I stop the ones I can."

Joel looked at the false troll's face. It was ugly, but not unkind. It seemed a much nicer face now than when he had first seen it.

"Now, after hearing all this, do you like me better?" Joel nodded slowly.

"Good, good. Now, I'll tell you my name. I'm Thumbor." As he said this he reached out to shake Joel's hand. Joel reached out too, and grasped Thumbor's hand. They shook. Joel's arm felt exactly as if it had been grabbed and swallowed by a bear. But Thumbor was smiling broadly as he let go. He said, "Let's have something to eat while I tell you why you are here."

The big man opened his large, green packsack. He fumbled around in it for a few moments and finally brought out a large chunk of bacon and a wedge of thick, yellow cheese. He also pulled out an iron pan and a long knife. He put the pan on the fire and gripped the knife purposefully.

He began talking again as he cut slices off the chunk of bacon and dropped them into the pan. "The old one, he came to talk to you?"

Joel said, "Do you mean Telmeer?"

"Yes." Thumbor picked up the cheese. "Telmeer is one of his names. Did he talk to you?"

"Yes."

"Well, he talked to me, too. In truth, he gave me the very most difficult assignment that I've ever had. He wants me to help you rescue a princess."

Joel blinked and said, "A princess!"

"Yes, I know, I know. It sounds very traditional, but it is true. Princesses in stories are always getting into trouble and being rescued by tall knights on fine horses. The truth of the matter is, though, that real princesses hardly ever need rescuing like that. They're guarded well and they can take care of themselves, too. That's one reason why our present problem is so sticky. The princess who we are going to try to help is far beyond the reach of any bumbling strongman in a suit of tin. Yes, indeed, she is being held by the Witch Queen." Thumbor paused to take a nip off a piece of the now sizzling bacon.

Joel was impressed. He thought for a moment and then asked, "Is it the same Witch Queen who cast a spell on you?"

Thumbor grunted (he had just burned his tongue on that nip of hot bacon) and growled, "Yes, yes, of course, there's only one, you know."

Joel said, "Oh."

Thumbor remained silent. He was busy putting good-smelling things on two large wooden plates. Joel looked around. He could see the first gray glow of dawn dimly outlining tall trees. Somewhere above, a bird sang a few sleepy notes and then snuggled again into silence.

Thumbor waved his knife toward the sunrise, "If I were a real troll I'd be nothing but a statue right now." He smiled. Joel couldn't help smiling back. Thumbor said, "That's better. We're going to have to trust each other if we're going to get through this adventure. It would be nice if we could have some fun doing it, too. Now, eat up while I tell you a few more important things. We have to get moving soon."

He thrust a plate at Joel. Joel began to eat. He started slowly but soon found that he was very hungry. Thumbor continued talking between mouthfuls. "Princess Meerlyn of Marl is the daughter of the King of Tananar. One day, while hunting near the edge of this forest, she was taken. I heard someone cry out and ran toward the sound. Behind remained five dead guards and one who was dying. The last guard was able to whisper a name to me before he, too, died. He said 'Dragonel.' "

Joel looked up from his plate, "What does that mean?"

Thumbor frowned, "It means trouble for us, Joel. Dragonel is the strongest, the biggest, the most evil of the western giants. His helpers are talking beasts who have gone bad. In his youth he was death to all who dared go near the far edge of this forest. Now, he is worse still; he is the Witch Queen's captain. He does her bidding and has her help. It was surely by her orders that he came so far from his home. By now, he has taken the Princess to his castle.

"A week ago talking wolves appeared at the gates of Marl. They carried a message from Dragonel. The message was a demand that a great treasure of gold and jewels be brought to the Plains of Morning by summer's end. The King is even now gathering the wealth of his kingdom. Somehow, the ransom will be paid."

Joel said, "Well, why must we do anything if the ransom is to be paid? Dragonel will give up Meerlyn, won't he?"

Thumbor smiled, "No, he won't. He won't. The Witch Queen won't let him. It is the thinking of the King and of Telmeer that the Witch Queen wants Meerlyn for some darker purpose. To be sure, the gold will be taken to the Plains of Morning. It will be offered. Very likely, Dragonel and his goblin soldiers will try to take it. There will be a great battle, but Meerlyn will not be saved by the fighting."

Joel said, "But what if the King's army wins the battle? Wouldn't that help?"

Thumbor looked up at the dark trees, "No. Dragonel will keep Meerlyn in his castle whatever happens. And that castle cannot be taken by storm. An ocean of blood would be spilled before even one of its stones could be moved. No, Meerlyn will be kept in the castle, or in the Witch Queen's tower above it. You must understand, Joel, the Witch Queen controls Dragonel, uses him as a tool in her foul plans."

Joel said, "Won't the Witch Queen accept some payment, some ransom? She must want something?"

Thumbor smiled grimly, "Yes, she wants everything—all power, all wealth—everything in Tananar. And she has no honor. She makes no bargains. She takes and gives only pain in return. She has no mercy. Ah, it was a cruel day when Meerlyn fell under the Witch Queen's hand! Evil greater than the loss of gold will come of it."

Joel could think of nothing to say. He scraped his plate with a crusty bit of cheese.

Thumbor sighed and said, "Joel, it's up to us. It's all up to us. We must seek out Meerlyn and help her to escape."

That summed it up simply, but Joel was sure that helping Meerlyn could prove to be pretty difficult. He asked, "How are we going to do it?"

Thumbor laughed. He had heard the doubtful tone in Joel's voice. He tapped his forehead and said, "I have a plan. I'll tell it to you when the time comes. Who knows? We may not even be able to use it."

Joel sat looking into the fire. The large man sounded much too cheerful about fighting magic animals and stealing princesses away from giants. Finally, Joel asked, "What will happen if your plan doesn't work?"

"Well," Thumbor grinned, "then we'll need some luck, some good thinking and we'll need Lor."

Joel looked at Lor where he had placed it against a broad tree root. There, it shone softly as if it held some secret of its own. Joel stared at it awhile and then put it in his pocket. Thumbor had already started to break camp. He scrubbed the dishes with handfuls of sweet-smelling pine needles. He looked at Joel and said, "Come, come, lend a hand. We've got to be traveling."

27

A few minutes later they had finished their chores and, except for a mound of sand over the fire's ashes, the little clearing looked as if they had never been there. Thumbor shouldered his pack and stepped between two large fir trees. Joel followed him and they walked together into the cool blueness of morning.

# III

## City of the Snails

By midday the two travelers found themselves beneath tall trees. Joel looked up in wonder. Sunlight gleamed through green clouds of leaves far above. Quiet, deeper than the sea, surrounded them.

Thumbor pointed toward the dim distance ahead of them, "Look, Joel! There is something you've never seen before."

Joel peered into the gloom. At first he could see nothing. After a few moments he could make out several slowly moving shapes. They were curved and very large, at least seven feet high. He said, "What are they?"

Thumbor said, "Snails. Giant snails."

Joel looked back at the curved shapes. Yes, he recognized them now. There were three of them. He could see their eye-stalks swaying as they moved. He shivered right down to his toes.

Thumbor said, "A little farther, in under the tallest trees, is their city. I've never seen it. It is said to be a strange, magical place."

Joel was curious. He wanted to get a look at the snails and their city. He said, "Let's go closer. I want to see them better."

Thumbor shook his head, "No, Joel, they don't like intruders. They keep to themselves. They have their secrets to guard."

Joel frowned, "But we could do it. They don't move fast. They could never catch us."

"Joel, that's not the point. They don't want us to look at them or bother them. This has long been known by travelers in the forest. The snails want us to pass quickly by. We should respect their wishes. Besides, they aren't as harmless as you think they are."

Joel said nothing and looked at the tops of his shoes.

Thumbor said, "Come on. I'm hungry. There's a stream just ahead. We can stop there for lunch and a nap." He turned and moved on through the green twilight. Joel followed him.

The stream was clear and cold. It flowed smoothly over small stairsteps of golden stone. The two travelers ate their lunch in silence. When they were done, Thumbor settled back against his pack and pulled his cap down over his eyes. Joel sat staring moodily into the stream.

"Why should I do what Thumbor says?" he thought. "It wouldn't hurt the stupid snails for me to look at them." He threw a pebble into the stream. "Who cares if they don't like to be bothered?"

Thumbor snored. Joel looked at him. The big man was sound asleep. Quietly Joel rose to his feet. The stream made soothing bell sounds. One step at a time Joel moved away from the circle of trees where they'd eaten their lunch. After twenty careful steps he turned and headed back toward the City of the Snails.

He frowned as he walked. Thumbor had told him not to bother the snails. But who was Thumbor to tell him what to do? Guilt like a thorn in his heart made him angry. He walked faster.

In a few minutes he reached the place where they had first seen the giant snails. He kept on without pausing.

Suddenly, he found himself staring down between his toes into a dark valley. Below the bluff all was quiet. Nothing moved. He stepped over the lip of the drop and began to climb down.

He soon found himself walking down a steep, broad path. Darkness became ever deeper as he went farther down. Any other time he would have been frightened. Stubborn anger kept him from feeling or thinking anything sensible.

The path broadened. He noticed that the slope became less steep. He rounded a large boulder and stopped short. Before him was the City of the Snails.

Smooth silver light flowed like water from the mouth of a vast cave. Wide terraces rose gently to meet the domed ceiling. Dozens of ramps led from terrace to terrace. Snails were everywhere. Because of the distance they seemed nearly of normal size.

Joel blinked. He saw many shapes which he did not recognize. The source of the silver light was a great waterfall at the very back of the cave. Somehow, light seemed to shine right through the water. Was there a star deep in the world's heart?

Below the waterfall was a lake. Around its edge plants were growing. Small birds flew between yellow flowers. Closer, blue spiders rested in webs of glowing gold.

There was a scratching noise behind Joel. He whirled around. Only a few feet away was a giant snail.

It was looking at him. Its eyestalks were even with his face. Its body was silver-gray. Its huge shell was gray shading to deep purple. It stayed very still.

A small click sounded to his right. He looked. Two more snails, smaller than the first one, had come from behind a boulder. He looked to his left. Three snails sat as still as stones watching him. He slowly turned toward the City of Snails. A dozen large snails were moving toward him through the silver light.

Joel turned to run back the way he had come. He raised his right foot and stopped. Slowly, he put it back down. Six more snails had joined the one who had first blocked his path. A wall of hard shells surrounded him. Eyestalks pointed stiffly at him. All of the snails began to close in, to slide towards him.

Joel remembered Lor. He reached into his shirt pocket. It was still there. He pulled it out and held it tightly in his hand. The snails were closer. He didn't know how to call upon the jewel's magic power. He had to try something before panic overcame him. He gripped Lor fiercely and ordered, "Kill them! Kill the snails! Kill them all!"

Nothing happened. The snails moved slowly, slowly closer.

Joel screamed, "Kill them!"

The snails stopped. Slowly their eyestalks turned away from Joel and pointed uphill. Joel looked above the back of the largest snails. He saw Thumbor. Thumbor was coming. Joel felt relief flood his heart.

The big man walked up to the edge of the ring of snails. One of the smaller snails moved aside to let him enter. Thumbor walked up to Joel and stood before him. Joel could see anger flashing in Thumbor's eyes. He didn't care. He was just glad to have his friend with him. Thumbor turned to face the largest snail. The snail watched the big man without moving.

Thumbor made a sweeping motion with his arms. The snail's eyestalks swayed slowly in reply. Thumbor's arms moved again. Joel's mouth opened with surprise. They were talking. The snail and Thumbor were speaking in a language of signs. For several moments the strange conversation continued.

Finally, Thumbor turned back to Joel and said, "This is the captain of the guard. Luckily, we've met each other before on its patrols far into the forest. We've met over two day's journey from here. Stand still. It wants to look at you."

The snail captain glided forward. It was now very close to Joel. Its eyestalks were no more than six inches from his nose. Joel looked up. The eyes were black beads, cold

*He gripped Lor fiercely and ordered,*
*"Kill them! Kill the snails!"*

and calm. They looked steadily into his own eyes. Joel felt as if he were being measured with a ruler. He lowered his head. He felt small and very, very weak.

The giant snail backed away from him. It made a sign with its eyestalks. Thumbor bowed low and walked between two snail guards. He turned and said, "Come on, Joel. And mind your manners."

Joel hesitated and then bowed to the snail captain. It gracefully lowered its eyestalks. Joel turned and followed Thumbor. He could feel the cool gaze of the snails on his back. Small hairs on his neck were tingling.

They said nothing as they walked back up the steep side of the valley. Joel kept his eyes on Thumbor's heels. His heart felt lighter and lighter with each upward step they took. Finally, they reached the top.

Thumbor didn't stop. He made directly for the place where they had eaten lunch. Joel said nothing and followed. The green light beneath the trees now seemed almost bright to him.

They reached the circle of trees. Thumbor knelt down and began putting their lunch things into his pack. Joel sat down on a rock next to the stream. He leaned over and put his face in the water. It was cold and sweet. He drank deeply.

He raised his head and found Thumbor looking at him. The big man said, "Joel, you did a foolish thing, a dangerous thing. If you do anything like this again, it could mean our lives. The snails are not enemies. They are just —different. We're both lucky that I've had some dealings with them before."

Joel said nothing and looked down. For half of a breath he nearly became angry. He almost spoke. Then, the memory of the snail captain's cold, black eyes came into his mind. He was silent. The memory would not leave him.

Thumbor said, "Trust me, Joel. Trust what I say. I need your trust and your help. We have far to go. Our enemies are cruel and will take joy in any mistake we make. We won't be able to make many of them."

Joel stared at the stream. He felt a hurt he had never known before—the disappointment of a friend. Thumbor was disappointed in him. This pain, like his memory of the snail captain, would not leave Joel when he willed it to go. It stayed, cutting at the hard places in his mind.

Thumbor finished packing. He rose and said, "Come on, Joel. We have miles to cover before we can sleep tonight." Joel got up and followed his friend into the deep places of the forest.

Silent, weary hours passed. In camp that night they did not speak. Joel was thinking. He thought longer and harder than he had ever thought before. The night was old before he finally slept.

# IV
## Gray Visitor

The following days were the most wonderful ones Joel had ever know.  They traveled swiftly.  Joel walked as much as he could, but he still spent a good bit of time riding in that large green pack on Thumbor's back.  They passed through deep forest — great round trunks with necklaces of pale ferns, clear drops of water gathered like crystals on the tips of dark leaves, cool quiet resting like a cloak over the shoulders of the trees.

Sometimes they would find clearings in the forest.  Then they would stop and rest on the soft meadow grass.  At these times, as well as at many others, Thumbor would teach Joel his woodland songs.  The words were hard for Joel to understand and the melodies were usually sad, but he liked them anyway.  Also, he never tired of hearing the strange tales that his large friend was always spinning.  This was true even though some were so wild and wonderful as to not mean a thing at all to Joel.  He did understand a few, though, and those which concerned giants gave him a special tingle.

On the sixth evening they made camp in a dark clearing.  Thumbor made a small fire and cooked their simple meal.  After the dishes were done and put away, he said, "Hey, Joel, catch."

Joel did and found that he was holding something yellow and sticky.  "What's this?" he asked.

"It's a candy, pitch and honey melted over a fire and left to harden for a week.  I made it just before you came.  It's good stuff.  Chew it."

Joel looked doubtfully at the lump he held in his hand.  "This isn't like those rotten mushrooms you got me to try yesterday, is it?"

Thumbor did his best to look shocked. "Joel! Would I do that twice to a friend? You spluttered and spit like a wet cat. Why, I was sorry I even saw the silly things. I wouldn't give you something bad-tasting again. Would I?"

Joel looked darkly at him. "You would if you thought you could get me to eat it."

Thumbor snorted, "Well, if that's the way you feel about it you can just go ahead and sit there. You won't know what you're missing." With that the big man popped a large gob of the stuff into his mouth and began to chew.

Joel carefully nibbled at a corner of the candy. It tasted good. He said, "It's sort of pepperminty."

Thumbor said, "Told you so."

Joel swallowed his candy and said, "Thumbor, how will the power of Lor help us?"

Thumbor looked at Joel, "What do you mean?"

Joel looked into the fire for a few moments and then said, "If we're in danger—say, the giant is going to grab us—how will Lor help?"

Thumbor said, "That can't be foretold."

Joel shook his head and said, "I don't think it will work. I don't think that there is any power in Lor."

Thumbor looked at him, "Why do you say that?"

Joel was quiet for several moments. Then, he said, "Back there with the snails, I tried to use Lor. I was frightened. I wanted to kill them, and I told Lor to help me. Nothing happened." Joel folded his hands.

Thumbor smiled a small smile and said, "Joel, you weren't in nearly as much danger as you thought you were. The snails would have carried you into their city and held you captive. They aren't violent. They seek only to mind their own business."

"Still," said Joel, "the power didn't come. I asked for help and nothing happened."

Thumbor said, "Joel, I know only a little about Lor's power. There is a wise person who knows much more than I do. You will soon meet her, I hope. Do you want me to tell you what I know anyway?"

Joel said, "Yes."

Thumbor sighed and said, "Telmeer told you the story about the great fish, didn't he?"

Joel nodded.

"Well," Thumbor said, "I know little more than that story. I do know that Lor is not like a tame dog. You can't call for Lor's help when you want it."

Joel said, "Then what good is it?"

"Patience, Joel, patience. The power is more like—like a friend. It will help you when you are in great need."

"When is that?"

"You can only partly be the judge of when you need Lor's help."

Joel said, "It would be more useful if you could use it when you wanted to."

Thumbor was silent for several moments. Finally, he said, "Joel, do you have whales in your world?"

"Yes. Why?"

"Imagine having a whale for a friend. You certainly couldn't order it around. It would use its great power to help you only because it liked you. In a strange way Lor's power is alive. It is far stronger than the strongest whale. And it knows when its strength needs to be used. At those times it will be ready. Do you understand?"

Joel shook his head and said, "Not really."

Thumbor looked down and said, "My words are clumsy. I don't understand Lor that well myself." He was quiet for a few moments. "There is one more thing. I know a a verse about Lor. It has a true sound to it. You should know it. Listen:

In seas of fear
With darkness near
Your strength is sand—
Only courage stands
And one thing more—
A star's bright heart—Lor

The verse is very old. It doesn't control Lor, but it does serve to guide you and it may even awaken the jewel's power when you are in great trouble."

Joel said the verse to himself several times. Finally, he looked at Thumbor, "I still don't really understand."

Thumbor shrugged, "That's all I know. Here, have another piece of candy."

They chewed in silence for awhile. Joel watched stars hide from the wind behind the branches of tall trees. He was beginning to feel very comfortable when Thumbor touched him lightly on the shoulder. Joel looked up. His friend's eyes were hard and bright.

"Joel, frown. Look miserable. And don't be surprised by anything that I say."

Joel said, "But, why . . ." and then thought better of saying anything else. Thumbor's face was grim.

The big man said, "Something, or somebody is watching us. There might be more, but I've only noticed one so far. We can't trust anyone we meet in this forest. We'll have to play a game. I'm going to be a real troll for awhile. You're my prisoner. Say nothing. Just act frightened of me. We must find out what the watcher wants." While he talked, Thumbor opened his pack and got out a thick piece of rope. He then began to tie Joel's hands together. Joel heard a twig snap. He looked up.

The wolf stood tall and open-mouthed just across the fire from him. It was no more than six feet away. Gray fur covered its large frame. Sparks of firelight glinted on its long teeth. Its eyes glowed orange behind the flames. It waited.

Thumbor calmly finished tying his knots (very loosely) and turned to face the wolf. He grunted " 'Lo, wolf. What do you want?" The wolf stared at Joel and said nothing. "Witch got your tongue? Or are you just some stray dog lost in the woods?"

The wolf spoke, "You know what I am, troll. And you'll soon know what I came for." Its words ended in a low, rough growl.

"I guess I will, now that you've kindly decided to talk." Thumbor's voice was like a sharp saw. "What did you come for, eh?"

"I'm on a mission for one whom you would do well to respect, troll. She has ears in this forest which help her to protect those who serve her. Unkind words earn rewards of fire." The wolf parted its jaws in an ugly smile.

Thumbor said, "Wolf, don't threaten me. I work for Dragonel. You still haven't told me what you want."

"My mission is my own—and the Queen's. What I want from you is the service you owe to her. I've traveled far and have farther yet to go. I need meat." The wolf looked hungrily at Joel. "Share with me your captive. I can run a week on the fruit of his bones."

"This manling belongs to Dragonel. It would be worth my head to kill him for supper. Go find a rabbit, wolf." Thumbor's hand rested lightly on his axe.

The wolf snarled and said, "My mistress sings the tune for your master, troll. If I say the boy belongs to me, he belongs to me. I can do what I want with him. Don't stand in my way."

Thumbor lifted his axe and said, "Argue with this, wolf." His face was still and hard like stone. The axe was steady in his hand.

The wolf stood ready to spring. Its eyes were flashing with hatred. Its teeth gleamed fiercely in a silent snarl. It leaped — and suddenly was gone into the darkness of the forest.

Joel began to breathe for the first time in many minutes. He looked at Thumbor. Thumbor turned and said, "Come, Joel. We've got to leave here now. That wolf is one of the Witch Queen's personal guards. It is probably setting out to alert her forces against any rescue parties that might be on the way to help the princess. Magic always leaves traces. The Witch Queen may soon learn of your arrival in our world."

Joel said, "How can it get word of us back to the Witch Queen?"

Thumbor was somber. "The Witch Queen has servants more swift and more evil than that one, Joel. And they are near. They are nearer than I like to think. Come, trolls are supposed to travel at night anyway. And," Thumbor smiled, "I know a trick or two that will soon have this wolf chasing its tail!"

They moved swiftly. Night and the forest covered them with a blanket of shadow. Joel, riding on Thumbor's back looked fearfully into the darkness behind them. He expected to see a pair of hungry, glowing eyes. The big man wove his way back and forth between trees. Once they splashed for what seemed like miles up a small stream. Another time Thumbor stopped in a dark glade and said, "I smell something we need." He rooted around for a few minutes before he finally straightened up. "This stuff will tickle the hairs off of any wolf's nose!" He held out a handful of pale, slender leaves. Joel sniffed and immediately began to sneeze. Thumbor chuckled quietly as he crushed the leaves and scattered them over their back-trail. They went on.

After many hours they came to a rocky place in the forest. The round boulders made Joel think of huge marbles. He didn't like to think about who might own such marbles. The sky was becoming violet when they settled down at last for a few hours of sleep.

# V

## A River Journey

Late on the seventh morning the land began to rise steeply in front of them. Thumbor remained quietly tense as they walked. His big hand was wrapped tightly around his axe. Joel glanced around nervously as they made their way over rough ground. He was still thinking about the wolf.

At noontime they came across a gently bubbling stream. Its ripples flashed silver-bright in the sunlight. Its green, peaceful depths calmed Joel, and washed away his shadowy fears of the previous night. Thumbor smiled widely when he saw the stream. Joel realized that they must have been searching for it. He was about to ask why, but Thumbor was already following the stream's course up into the rising hills. Joel had to run to catch up.

Two hours of rough hiking brought them to a place which Joel could never have imagined if he had tried for a hundred years. They had just finished climbing some stairstep rocks beside which the stream plunged over a small falls. They now stood at the top of the falls in a cut between two tall cliffs. Before them lay a deep, smooth pool of water. Thumbor bent down, reached into the water, grasped a hidden rope, and began pulling. He tugged on the dripping rope. From behind a large rock a very small raft emerged. Soon, Thumbor had it bobbing beside them. The raft was made of bark-covered logs held together by vines, and it looked none too sturdy. Thumbor motioned for Joel to climb on. This Joel did with a good deal of caution. The raft felt even less sturdy than it looked when Thumbor hopped on next to Joel. Then the big man untied the rope and the raft drifted slowly away from the lip of the falls.

*Beneath the raft swam several dozen bright, blue fish.*

Joel, sure now that the raft wasn't about to sink, began to look around. On either side of him golden cliffs rose straight up for at least three hundred feet, but the pool itself was no more than forty feet wide. In front of him it curved around a turn in the narrow canyon. The water was very still. Only a few small ripples flew like flights of birds across the surface. Sunshine beat warmly down on them as they moved steadily further from the falls. Thumbor, who was sitting quietly by Joel's side, lifted his hand to scratch a large, red ear. Suddenly, Joel looked at him. Thumbor looked back and grinned. He had guessed what Joel was thinking and was silently asking why Joel hadn't thought of it before. They had begun to move quite swiftly. How? How, indeed! Thumbor, still grinning, pointed into the water. Joel looked over the knobby side of the raft and got one of the surprises of his life.

Beneath the raft swam several dozen bright, blue fish. Each one held a leather thong in its mouth. The thongs were attached to the underside of the raft. Obviously, the fish were pulling the little craft upstream. Joel looked back at Thumbor. "Do they know you?" he asked.

Thumbor laughed and said, "Yes, in a way they do. Their mistress knows me and she has told them to help us. It's a good thing, too. We're safe here."

Joel peered curiously into the water again. Each fish was slim and very powerful looking. None of them paid the slightest attention to him. He peered past them, trying to see down to the bottom. He couldn't. He leaned forward. His eyes fell farther and farther into midnight mistiness.

Thumbor's big hand on Joel's belt saved him from falling in. "Not yet, not yet! You'll get a chance to swim soon enough. Just wait awhile my fine, fat fish. Just wait!" Joel turned bright red.

This made Thumbor laugh thunderously.

Anger exploded within Joel and he shouted, "Don't laugh at me! I don't like it! I'm not a fat fish. You're the one who should be laughed at. You're the ugly one."

Thumbor looked surprised and then hurt. After a moment or two he said, "I meant nothing by it, Joel, nothing. Forget I said it."

Joel knew that he'd been wrong, but that only upset him more. He just sat still on the front of the raft and stared furiously into the water. Thumbor said nothing and looked straight ahead.

After a half hour of twisting turns their raft glided gently to a stop. The tips of the logs came to rest on fine, gray sand. Thumbor got to his feet and stepped lightly onto the beach. Joel looked over the edge of the raft; the blue fish were gone.

Keeping his eyes down, he, too, stepped from the raft. Thumbor took off his pack and bent to open it. Joel looked quickly around. He saw that they were in a hollowed out **place at the base of the eastern cliff. It held the sandy** beach, a little soil, and three small, good-smelling pine trees. The nearby cliff rose a frightening distance into the sky. Joel looked down again.

At this moment a thought came into Joel's mind. It was a new thought, and, as is the way with such thoughts, it was very clear. He knew for the first time that he really didn't enjoy being angry. The reasons why this was so are important, of course, but they didn't come to him until much later. He only knew that he didn't want to be angry with Thumbor. All his bad feeling left him, and before he quite knew what he was doing he said, "Thumbor." The big man turned around. "Thumbor, I'm sorry for what I said. I shouldn't have gotten angry like that. I'm sorry." Joel waited.

An afternoon breeze began to nose at his cheek like a curious puppy. He slowly raised his eyes to look at Thumbor. His gaze met a wide smile. And the smile was in the

45

man's eyes and seemed, somehow, to be coming from all over him. Joel had become embarassed about his apology, but Thumbor's smile told him that that was as silly as being angry in the first place. He smiled back.

Thumbor laughed long and loudly and finally said, "Joel, Joel, let's make some noise, for now's the last time that we'll feel safe enough to yell."

Joel looked around doubtfully as the echoes of Thumbor's voice bounded away down the canyon. "Why are we safe here? It almost seems as if we're trapped."

Thumbor winked and said, "Well, we could be trapped if a certain somebody said that she wished it to be so. But we're not. And later you may discover more about why we are safe."

He smiled mysteriously. Then, with a sudden motion, Thumbor seized Joel and lifted him high in the air, then threw him out over the water.

Joel shouted as the smooth, blue pool rose swiftly to meet him. After a most satisfying smack he sank into the cold water. When he reached the surface again he saw Thumbor charging through the pool like a frisky whale. For the next few minutes they had a splash fight. The battle ended in a dripping, laughing draw.

They both tumbled ashore and flapped their arms wildly in an effort to shake off loose water. Then, they sat down in the sand. They dried in the warm sun. Soon, they fell asleep.

# VI

## Queen Pellin

Joel woke up and stretched. Thumbor was sitting beside him. The big man seemed to be sewing something. Joel turned to him and said, "Let's have dinner. We missed lunch and I'm hungry."

Thumbor looked at his work and said, "Unless I miss my guess, you're going to be asked out to dinner." He laughed at Joel's bewildered expression and pointed toward the water. "Ah, here comes your invitation now."

Joel turned his head and, at first, saw nothing. His eyes slowly became used to the light reflected off the stream. He saw one of the bright, blue fish. It was floating motionless near the shore and it held something in its mouth. Thumbor put his hand in the water. The fish remained calm and still. Slowly Thumbor extended his fingers and took a package from the fish's mouth. Joel heard, but did not see the fish whirl and dive back into deep water. His eyes were on the package.

It was a tiny box, but such a box! It was made of the warmest gold and its lid was a clear, blue sapphire. Thumbor worked the golden catch and the sapphire swung up. Inside was a fine brilliant powder. Joel couldn't say what color the powder was. It seemed to be all colors at once and none in particular. He looked at Thumbor.

Thumbor had a thoughtful expression on his face as he began to speak, "Joel, you have a chance now to meet a very special creature. Few have met her. I, myself, have spoken with her only once. She wants to meet you and talk with you. However, it will take a bit of what you would call magic to enable you to make the visit. For the magic to work you will have to trust its maker. That's me. There is some danger in it. There always is with magic. Will you take the chance?"

Joel was nervous, but he didn't think twice about his answer, "Yes, I'll take it," he said, "Just tell me what to do."

Thumbor smiled and said, "You are going to meet a queen. Mind your manners and think carefully about what you say. Now, I'm going to sprinkle some of this powder on you, but first you must get into the water."

Joel walked into the water until it was up to his waist. Thumbor followed him. "Good! I'll tell you when to start. When I do, duck your head under the water; count to ten; and then take a deep breath. Got that?"

Joel gave Thumbor a questioning look, but nodded yes. Thumbor poured the shining powder from the box into the cup formed by his left hand. He raised his hand high and said, "Begin."

As he ducked under water Joel saw a wonderful rainbow of color spring from his friend's fingers. He almost forgot to count, but he remembered in time to start on four. When he got to ten he took a deep, deep breath, and . . .

And he tasted cool, rich air. He had expected, as you can guess, to get a throatful of choking water. He opened his eyes (which somehow had become tightly shut) and looked out upon a twilight landscape. It was then that he understood. He was still under water. He was breathing water. This was the magic.

Joel was still blinking and looking around when a voice sounded behind him, "You are the walker called Joel?" Joel turned his head and saw a large fish. It was much darker than the raft-pullers had been. Also, it was looking right at him.

"Are you Joel?" Joel managed to nod yes. The fish spoke again, "Then, come with me. You have much to do and the magic will end in a few hours."

Joel hesitated.

"Come," said the fish, "my name is Rainbow. We must go."

Joel now found that the magic had also given him the power to swim very fast. He had no trouble at all in keeping up with his guide.

They passed into deep water. Soon, they were over the deepest section of the pool. Rainbow turned his face from the sun and dove downwards. Joel followed. They swam down for a long time. He couldn't tell how long, but no color remained in the water. Blackness surrounded them on all sides. Joel began to be a little afraid. It was then that he saw the lights.

Imagine, if you can, being out where night begins, out where there is nothing but darkness. Imagine being there and seeing all of the sky's stars spread below you like a field of snow. Imagine coming down to the snow-stars, falling in among them, seeing them change into sparks of color— red, gold, green, and silver. Imagine all of this and you will know something of what Joel saw as he came to the bottom of the pool.

In fact, he stopped and stared while Rainbow swam on. He found that the lights weren't stars after all, but small glowing shells. He saw that he wasn't alone. Hundreds of fish, scales shining in the clear light, watched him from a distance. Suddenly, Rainbow returned and made an impatient motion with his tail. Once again, Joel followed.

They soon came to the entrance of a cave. It was guarded by the two largest crabs that Joel had ever seen. Their claws could easily have snipped off his arm. They sat still as stone. The two swimmers passed between them.

Joel now found himself in a long passageway. The walls on either side were decorated with pictures of water animals. They looked real. Joel began to wonder if they even were pictures. Rainbow never gave him a chance to stop and check, however. At last, they reached a door.

What looked to be one door was actually two doors. Attached to each door by a golden harness was a fish. The two fish wore black and white markings, and both had very somber expressions on their faces. Joel got the feeling that they were quite old. Rainbow made a low whistling sound. It must have been a password. The two gatekeepers strained at their harnesses. Slowly, the great doors swung outwards. Before they were completely open, Rainbow slipped between them. Joel followed. In this way he entered the castle of the Queen of the Rivers and Rains.

Joel found himself alone in a large hall. Tall arches of orange coral were lit by more of the shining shells. Rainbow had disappeared. Large pearls and blue jewels of the sea hung in clusters on the walls to either side. Pale, green water plants floated high above like flags. Before him stood a tall table made of pearl. As he stared at the table the light-shells got much brighter. Someone else came into the hall.

The Queen was much smaller than Joel had thought she would be—only four feet long. Her scales were dark blue above shading to silver-blue below. Her eyes were golden with large, dark pupils. Her fins, and especially her tail, were long and graceful. She looked at Joel for a moment. He bowed to her without thinking. With a flick of her tail she was beside the pearl table. Joel swam up beside her.

She watched him for several moments while he became quite nervous. Not many people, after all, are used to being closely inspected by a fish. Finally, she spoke, "Welcome, friend of Telmeer! Your name is Joel?"

"Yes, Joel Burnham." As he spoke Joel felt that his voice sounded very small.

"Twice welcome, Joel Burnham! I am Queen Pellin." She waited a moment and then went on. "Joel, I am glad to meet you. Thumbor has brought you here through

50

*Not many people, after all, are used to being closely inspected by a fish.*

great danger. When you leave, you will pass into greater danger still." Her voice was clear and bright like brook water. "Telmeer also had something to do with your being here. You must have many questions about what has happened to you. If you like, I will try to answer them."

Joel blinked. She expected him to say something. Instead, he turned red. Her eyes sparkled in what Joel took to be a smile. He was sure it wasn't a hurtful sort of smile. At last he managed to say, "Yes, I was confused at first." He paused and thought.

"In truth, I'm still confused. But so much has happened that I haven't had time to straighten it all out. I have never had a thing to do with magic before. And this place seems to run on magic. It seems right to be talking to you; but, if I told someone in my world about it, they would say I was a liar. I'm still not sure that this all isn't some sort of dream." Joel stopped for breath.

Queen Pellin said, "Dreams are not always what you think they are, Joel. You are really here, though. And this world is very different from yours. For one thing, Tananar is very, very old. It is old enough to be a grandmother to your world." She stopped and stared at him. "You look as if you don't think that this small history lesson is important."

Joel moved uncomfortably and said, "Why should it be?"

The Queen thought for awhile and said, "Have you ever seen water and sand mixed together in a glass jar?" Joel nodded.

"Good. At first, when it's all shaken up, the mixture is cloudy. Slowly, slowly the sand drifts downward and settles on the bottom of the jar. When enough time has passed the water is left clear. Worlds are like jars of water and sand. New ones are all shaken up, cloudy. Evil and good are mixed together in everything. Your world is like this. No person in your world can be all good, or all bad—though

52

some come close to being one or the other. In Tananar much time has passed and the waters are clear. There are good creatures. And there are evil ones. We fight those who dwell in darkness. You have come here to help us in our fight against those evil ones."

Joel said, "Thumbor told me that the Witch Queen ordered Dragonel to take Princess Meerlyn. What does the Witch Queen want with her? Why is Meerlyn so important?"

Queen Pellin moved closer to the pearl table. She said, "Joel, let me tell you a bit more about the Witch Queen. She is a magnet to all evil beings. She has become their leader. She gives purpose to their acts. From her mind come plans of conquest and enslavement. She won't be satisfied until she rules everyone, every living thing. Thumbor may have told you something about her."

Joel nodded, "He told me a little."

Queen Pellin raised her eyes, "She has a grand plan. Meerlyn is at the center of this plan. The Witch wants to take Marl. If she could capture the city, she would gain control of this half of the world. As you know, Meerlyn's father, the King of Tananar, rules from Marl. He protects the city and the wide lands around it. It is the heart of his kingdom. After he dies Meerlyn will be Queen.

"In a year's time the Witch will ride at the head of a large army. Even now, she is away gathering wicked creatures to her flag. She will try to take Marl by fire and storm. At her side will be Meerlyn."

Joel said, "What? How can that be? I don't know her, but surely Meerlyn wouldn't fight against her own father. She wouldn't help the Witch Queen. Would she?"

"No," said Queen Pellin, "she wouldn't. If she had a choice."

Joel swallowed and said, "Doesn't she?"

"Joel, the Witch Queen is very powerful, very evil. She

knows all the ways of giving pain. Meerlyn is strong and good. But the Witch will twist her, twist her. In the end she will have no choice. She will be the Witch's tool. She will ride against her own father."

Joel said, "Would she know what she would be doing?"

"Yes. That's the terrible part. She would know. But she would be helpless. She wouldn't be able to stop herself. She would help the Witch conquer her own country. Then, she would rule it as the Witch's puppet. She must be saved from doing this."

Joel nodded, "Thumbor is right. I see now why gold won't get her back."

Queen Pellin said, "Fortunately, the Witch Queen's **greatest hope did not come true. She did not get Lor.**"

Joel's head jerked up.

"Yes," said the Queen, "all who have knowledge, including the Witch, thought Lor would go to Meerlyn. It came to you instead."

Joel said, "But I thought Telmeer said that only I could use Lor's power. Why would the Witch Queen want it?"

"Joel, any great power can be used for good or for evil. The Witch Queen would seize Lor. It would burn her, wither her, but she would hold it. She would suffer greater pain than you can imagine. In the end, though, she would bend Lor to her will. Her magic power would then be twice as great as it was before."

Joel said, "Could she take Lor from me?"

"Ah, yes. She could. And she certainly will try if you meet her. I hope you don't! Lor would try to protect you. I can't say who would win. It would be a terrible battle."

Joel looked at Queen Pellin. She had turned. Her graceful tail stretched out behind her. She went on, "Fighting is wrong, Joel. Don't misunderstand me. It should be done only in defense of someone's life, of someone's freedom. In this world it is sometimes easier to tell who should be fought than it is in your world. Still, you must be very careful." She paused. After a moment she said, "Do you have any other questions?"

Joel breathed in deeply. Queen Pellin's words sounded like some fairy tale, but they were true. Meerlyn's life, and a great deal more, depended on what he and Thumbor could do to help her. He said, "Thumbor tried to tell me about Lor, but I still don't know how to use its power. Can you tell me what I should do, how I am to use it?"

Queen Pellin said, "Lor found you. It needs you so that its magic will be complete. It will be yours until you die. You and Thumbor will probably need its power before you are through with this adventure. Remember, the jewel can be a powerful weapon. It can also be a healing tool. Use it wisely when the times comes."

Joel was suddenly angry. "How? How? I don't know a thing about magic! I have Lor, but I don't know how to use it. What do I do? When do I do it?"

"Joel," the Queen's voice was kind, "you will use Lor when your need is very great. I can't tell you how to control it. I don't know. No one does—except the Witch. You and the jewel fit each other. Do you tell your hat to turn away raindrops?"

"No."

"The power is something like that. When you need it, it will be there. Did Thumbor tell you the old verse?"

"Yes."

"Please say it for me," Queen Pellin smiled.

Joel thought for a moment and then said:

> In seas of fear
> With darkness near
> Your strength is sand—
> Only courage stands
> And one thing more—
> A star's bright heart — Lor

55

Joel looked down. Queen Pellin's voice sounded close beside him, "Well said, Joel Burnham, well said! Trust Thumbor. Trust Lor. Follow your adventure to its end."

There was a long silence. Finally, Joel smiled, "I still don't understand, but I'll try."

The Queen said, "I know you will. Know, too, that all creatures of the water are your friends. We will help you if we can."

Joel knew that he had been given a promise. He smiled again and said, "Thank you, Queen Pellin."

She looked at him with a question in her eyes. "Joel, I wish a favor from you. May I see Lor? It was one of my kind that brought it to this world long ago."

Joel said nothing. Slowly he removed the jewel from his pocket and held it before the Queen. It gleamed softly golden. Queen Pellin's eyes took on some of its light. She whispered, "Yes, it has great beauty — and power." She turned quickly away and was quiet for many moments.

Joel remained standing with the jewel in his hands. He began to understand. He looked into the glowing jewel. Lor was indeed powerful and its power could affect his friends as well as his enemies. He felt that the jewel was pulling him onward — yet its light was pale and clear . . . and held no shadows. Shrugging, he put it back in his pocket.

Queen Pellin turned toward him, "Forgive me, Joel. Your time here is short and my hospitality has been less than it should be. Let us begin the feast."

A bell rang somewhere near. Long-legged lobsters and red seahorses carried in trays of food. Joel tried everything. He never seemed to get full. Some of the things he ate were most strange. Some tasted so good that he never wanted to stop eating them. The music of bells surrounded him. Others came.

An octopus as large as a small truck spoke to him about sea dragons. A graceful salmon asked him questions

56

about horses. It had seen their legs in streams, but it could never get a clear look at their bodies. All were very curious about the world of air.

A dance began. All of the creatures in the hall started to move slowly around each other. Joel's eyes were filled with moving lights and cloudy shapes. The dancers moved faster and faster. Suddenly, it was over. Joel knew that it was time for him to go.

Queen Pellin came up to him. Two seahorses carried something before her. It was a long slender package wrapped in dark blue. She spoke kind words of farewell and gave him the blue-wrapped package. It was heavy. He took it sleepily and thanked her.

Rainbow took him again through the jeweled halls. They passed the giant crabs. He remembered looking down one last time upon the shining galaxy of shells.

The magic ended when he broke through to the surface. He stumbled out of the water and fell into Thumbor's arms. He was so tired. Thumbor carried him to a bed of warm sand. He slept long and deeply.

# VII

## Pit of Spears

Joel woke up wondering where he was. He fuzzily remembered getting out of the water. Sleepily, he squinted into into bright, morning sunshine.

"Good morning, sleeping ugly!"

Joel faced the sound of Thumbor's voice. "You should talk!"

"Enough of your sharp tongue. Come, dull it on some breakfast. We have traveling to do."

Joel pulled himself up. Thumbor had been busy. The Queen's subjects had brought him the makings of a second feast—orange and yellow and purple fruits from the Queen's garden, green grasses gathered from the deepest lakes, ice-blue confections of a mysterious nature. He had made a giant's breakfast. Joel couldn't remember when he had been hungrier. Both of them fell to eating. They continued until there was nothing left.

"Now," said Thumbor, "we must be off. Today's raft ride will be our last day of travel in sunlight. I must begin to live up to my reputation as a troll. After today we must walk at night. Start packing!"

Joel knelt down beside his blanket and began to roll it up. He stopped. The Queen's gift was lying unopened on the sand. He had forgotten it. Slowly he picked it up. The blue covering was actually some kind of reptile skin. But each scale was as big as a saucer. Joel didn't want to know what kind of creature had originally owned the skin. A leather thong held the package shut. He pulled it and the covering fell away.

"Thumbor!"

"What, Joel? I'm just . . . ahh! I see you've gotten around to opening it."

"Thumbor, it's beautiful." On the smooth skin lay a shining sword. Its hilt was gold. Its pommel was one large emerald. The blade was slender and very sharp. It was just the right length for Joel.

"Yes, the Queen figured that you might need something more than your pretty face to get you through this adventure."

"It's mine?"

"It's yours."

"I didn't thank her nearly enough." The emerald looked as if it were alive. It caught and held the morning sun. "This stone must be priceless. I . . . I can't take it."

"It's yours, Joel. It does no good sitting in Queen Pellin's treasury. Such an object is worth no more than its use. You need the sword. Use it well!"

"I must thank her again!"

"She knows. Put it on."

With fumbling fingers Joel fastened the sword belt around his waist. He looked once again at the shining blade and then slid it smoothly into its scabbard. He looked up.

Thumbor grinned, "It's a good morning for gifts. Here," the big man handed him something made of soft leather, "it's a pouch. You can put Lor in it."

Joel smiled. He took out Lor and slipped it into the pouch. He then placed the long thong over his head and put the pouch inside his shirt. "Thanks, Thumbor!"

"Nothing to it, Joel. Come on! We have little time. Onto the raft with you!"

They threw their things onto the logs and got on. The raft immediately began to move. For many minutes Joel could not take his eyes off the sword in its scabbard.

When Thumbor finished arranging their gear, he turned to Joel. "Well," he said, "what did Queen Pellin have to tell you?"

Joel, still fingering the hilt of the sword, said, "She told

59

me a little about Lor and quite a lot about Meerlyn. That girl is truly in trouble. It sounds like we'll be joining her soon. I hope we can help her."

Thumbor looked down, "I hope so, too. I hope so."

Joel looked at the big man, "Do you know her?"

"Yes," Thumbor looked up, "very well. She saved my life once."

Joel stared at the hard muscles of Thumbor's arms. He was stronger than three men put together. "How could a princess ever save you?"

Thumbor smiled, "It was five years ago. She was only nine years old. I was in a town called Tullyman. It's by the sea. The people there are mostly fisherfolk. Every year they have a big celebration when the far-voyagers come home. I was there to gather information about the western ocean where the islands of the wizards lie. Those fisherfolk are wise and they see much that is useful.

"Well, I was careless. I had almost forgotten that I do look like a most ferocious troll. Because I had been around during the day, I thought that the people had become used to seeing me. I was wrong. Darkness and firelight, it seems, make me look far worse than I really do.

"There is a great bully in Tullyman named Trigo. This fellow is very brave with a crowd at his back. I was sitting in the courtyard of the Blueberry Inn having my supper— a very good supper it was, too. This Trigo tripped and spilled his pot of beer on my head. Quite naturally, I told him that he had been impolite. When I put him down on the ground once again, he seemed upset. He ran off, though, so I returned to my supper.

"Soon, too soon for me, he came back. He had about fifty angry fishermen with him. He had told them that he had been attacked by a troll. They were only too ready to believe Trigo's story. They were all feeling wild to begin with. I suppose I would feel wild if I'd been at sea for three months.

60

"Anyway, after a bit of hurly and burly, I found myself tied to a large post. Those fisherfolk who were not holding their heads in their hands were piling branches and sticks around my feet. Yes, they were going to roast me—an acceptable method of getting rid of unwanted trolls, if one is in a hurry. It looked bad for me.

"Then, Meerlyn came. She had been at the celebration of the returning boats that morning. I suppose her father had asked her to represent him. She gave a gift of gold and flowers to the captain of the fleet. Perhaps she had seen me standing at the edge of the crowd—in bright sunlight. Somehow, she knew I was no troll.

"Trigo had a torch in his hand. He was grinning at me. Just as he was about to thrust the flame under my feet, Meerlyn stepped forward. Without a word she climbed up on the pile of branches in front of me. She stood there and faced the crowd. At first, there were angry shouts. Soon, though, they saw who she was and quieted down. Only then did she speak.

"She said, 'This man is no troll. Did you not see him in sunlight this morning?'

"Trigo shouted, 'Burn him! Kill him! He's a troll!'

"Before anyone else could shout, Meerlyn said, 'Alright. We'll leave him for the sun to kill. There's no harm in that. I will stand here and guard him until dawn breaks. Wait here with me, if you wish.' "

Thumbor was quiet for a moment. He turned and looked into Joel's eyes, "They didn't dare to move her, not the King's daughter. The crowd stood about muttering for a moment and then began to scatter. Most went on to their homes. A few of the roughest stayed. Two of the King's guards were near, and, in front of me, Meerlyn. She stood right there until the rising sun shone full on my face. A troll would have withered. Meerlyn smiled. Then she took a knife from one of the guards and cut my bonds. Trigo and his friends drifted away like the cowards they were. A little girl had saved my life."

They were both quiet for awhile. Joel listened to the gentle song of the river. Finally, he asked, "Did you ever see her again?"

Thumbor looked up, "Yes. Many times. I have showed her some of the secrets of the forest. We are friends and I will not let the Witch Queen hurt her."

Joel looked into the big man's eyes. A silent promise passed between them—Meerlyn would be saved if either of them lived to reach her.

They followed the windings of the river for the rest of the day. The ride was smooth and quiet. Joel watched the team of blue fish for awhile. Soon, he became sleepy. He pillowed his head against Thumbor's pack as the raft floated into a wide pool.

Thumbor said, "No naps now, Joel. Here's where we go to work." Joel raised his head reluctantly and sat up. The raft glided across the pool and nosed gently against a sandy bank. Sunset was near as they gathered their things and stepped onto the shore. Thumbor turned to the pool and waved. Joel saw a huge, dark shape move into the shadow of deep water. He looked questioningly at Thumbor. Thumbor said, "Yes. We weren't alone. You didn't think Queen Pellin would let us travel unguarded did you?"

Joel said, "What was that?"

Thumbor smiled, "A friend . . . and thank your stars for that!"

They began walking up a steep trail. It was the first of many hard climbs they made during that night. Just before dawn they crossed a high, narrow pass. In the morning light Joel found himself looking down upon a land of ashen hills. He could feel heat rising from them. Thumbor had told him that those hills would turn hard and red in the sunlight. They had reached the desert called Bren. It marked the border of the Witch Queen's realm. Quickly,

62

they found a narrow cave in which they could pass the day. It was too hot to sleep, too hot to talk, too hot even to think. Joel lay watching grayish ants troop wearily across the cave's floor. Finally, in spite of the heat, he slept. His weariness was so great that he did not even hear Thumbor's thunderous snoring.

Hours of burning light passed. They came out of their cave as soon as the sun went down. They began walking. The path wound around crumbling boulders. Before many hours had passed they were down among the red hills. It was still terribly hot. Thumbor and Joel didn't talk as they moved slowly ahead on the stony trail. Thumbor was leading when they found him.

"Stop!"

"What's the matter?" said Joel.

"Shhhh!!!!"

"But . . ."

"There's something ahead. Stay here." Thumbor walked carefully forward. He waited. He motioned for Joel to come to him.

"Look, a trap."

Joel stepped to his side. In front of them was a black hole. Thumbor knelt and began pushing dirt aside with his hands. He uncovered rough, straw mats. He lifted the edge of the closest one and began to pull it away from the hole. A low snarl came from below them. The snarl ended in a strangled cough.

Thumbor said, "The victim lives. It's a good thing he came this way before we did. I might have plunged into this with my toes. We may yet be able to help him."

They moved the rest of the dirt and the mats. The trap was laid bare. A deep pit had been dug in the trail. It was several feet wide and ten feet long. Sticking up from the bottom of the pit were dozens of sharpened sticks. They were cruel and curved like a snake's fangs. Wedged among them was a wounded fox.

63

Thumbor said, "Fox, hear me. We won't hurt you. We want to help you."

The fox growled weakly, "Stay back, troll. You want to help me into your stomach. Stay back."

Thumbor said, "I'm going to lower this boy. He'll bring you up." The fox growled again, but said nothing more.

Joel said, "Shall I tie him?"

Thumbor said, "No, he's too weak to hurt you. Take the small water-skin and give him a drink. See how badly he's wounded." Joel nodded.

Thumbor tied a rope around Joel's waist. Joel eased himself over the edge of the pit. He shivered when he looked down and saw the ugly stakes waiting for him. He decided not to look down again. Thumbor slowly lowered him until his feet were just above the sharp points.

"Alright, Joel, see if you can kick some of those spikes out of your way. Beware of poison on the tips."

Joel gingerly placed his feet against one of the stakes. He pushed with all of his strength. It moved, but he moved too. He found himself swinging across the pit like an old clock's pendulum. He banged against the wall and stopped. He braced himself for another try. This time he bent the stick clear over. Thumbor dropped him into the place where it had been. Joel pushed two other sticks down. He was finally able to turn to the fox.

The fox raised his head. His eyes were dull. His tongue was dry and dark red. Joel opened the skin and poured some water into his cupped hand. The fox tried to move. Joel leaned over and held his hand below the fox's muzzle. The fox lapped weakly at the water. Joel now saw a nasty cut which ran along one side of the animal's body. He could see no other wounds. He guessed that the fox was suffering mostly from heat and thirst.

Something bumped Joel on the shoulder. It was a food sack. He looked up. Thumbor was pointing toward the fox. Joel nodded. Slowly he reached out to touch the red back. Yellow eyes cleared and looked into his. He didn't blink. Gently Joel began to stroke the soft fur. Yellow eyes closed. Joel carefully slid the sack beneath the fox's body. He cradled the fox in the sack and held him close. Thumbor began to pull on the rope. Joel and the fox were swiftly raised from the pit of spears.

Joel steadied himself on the pit's edge and looked up at Thumbor. Thumbor raised his finger to his lips. Joel nodded. The big man carefully picked out a path around the cruel pit. He reached safe ground, turned and motioned to Joel. Joel looked briefly at the dazed fox in his arms and then followed.

# VIII
## The Monster's Cave

An hour before dawn they came to a cave. Its entrance was narrow. Splintered rocks rose high above it and merged into the torn flank of a hill. Thumbor went in first. Joel followed, carrying the fox. A horrible smell rose from the darkness and nearly knocked him over. He gagged and his eyes filled with tears. Thumbor pulled a pitch-splinter from a pocket in his pack and lit it. Red light flickered across the cave's rough floor. They saw death.

The orange and ivory gleam of gnawed bones picked at their eyes. Thumbor's face was grim. Most of the bodies were those of small animals. One or two had once been human.

Thumbor said nothing. He went deeper into the cave. Joel stumbled after him. The smell faded as they walked down a narrow tunnel. The air became very cold and damp. Finally, they arrived at the shore of an underground lake. Its waters spread far beyond the dim light of the torch.

Joel put the fox down on the sandy shore. He looked back toward the cave's entrance and said, "Thumbor, what was that place back there?"

Thumbor started. He had been thinking. "That place is the lair of a fire-bat. It's one of the Witch Queen's favorite pets. I'd thought that we could get through these hills without meeting one. It's out hunting now, and scouting. If it had been at home when we walked in, we would now be dead."

Joel was shocked. "Why did we come down here? Why didn't we run?"

Thumbor smiled grimly, "I've made a mistake, a bad one. When I was here just three years ago, this cave was safe. Tonight I thought only of our need for good water.

I didn't take precautions, check for signs. Now . . . running will do us no good. We've tramped on the beast's front doorstep. It will smell our trail. And this bat can fly further in an hour than we can run in a day. It will search us out wherever we try to hide. It is better to meet it here. We have to kill it—if we can."

Joel felt cold inside. He'd never seen Thumbor look so grave. "What should we do?"

Thumbor said, "When it comes, we must surprise it. We must fool it. I will act like a very proud, very stupid troll. You must sit against the wall. Pretend that you are dazed and frightened. Hold onto your sword, but keep it hidden beside you. I'll talk with the fire-bat and make it angry. It will go for me and when it does you must cut it from behind. Watch out for its fangs, Joel. A scratch from them will kill you."

Joel swallowed and said, "What if I miss?"

Thumbor looked at him calmly, "Then I'll have a smaller chance of living through the fight."

There was a long silence. Then Thumbor smiled. Joel tried to smile back. Thumbor reached over and held his shoulder tightly. "Hit it hard, Joel, and then I'll kill it. Come, we must be ready. Sit over here. I'll get back by the water."

Joel felt the cold stone against his back. He looked at the fox. The animal was still too weak to understand what was happening. Thumbor was busy assembling a small, oil stove. That was part of the plan. He wanted to look like a troll cooking supper.

Waiting. Joel listened to the faroff sound of waterdrops falling on stone. He tried not to think about what was coming. Fear was like sand in his eyes. He was afraid of failing his friend. The big man trusted him. He must not fail that trust. He feared the unseen beast. He thought of softly shining bones. This was to be a true fight, a fight for life. He knew now that he would never fight just for fun again. He would never fight for false pride. He would never take joy in causing others to hurt. He would never— if he got the chance. His life could be ended in the coming battle.

Water fell on stone. Joel wished that it could be over. He squeezed the pommel of his sword. There was a movement of air. He jerked his eyes toward the tunnel entrance The fire-bat was there.

Joel knew what it was to be really afraid. The great bat's wings beat slowly against the thick air. Its body was covered with grey fur. Hooked claws curved down from its feet. Long fangs stood out from its mouth. The flame of Thumbor's torch flickered in its eyes.

"SSSSSS—SSSSSSSSSS–sssssss . . . What do you want, Troll?" Its voice was soft and dead like closet dust.

Thumbor's voice was gruff when he spoke, "I only want shelter from the sun, little bat."

"Ts–s–s–s–s–ssssss." The fangs glowed flame-bright. "No insults, troll. You know what I can do to you."

The small head turned to Joel. He felt blood drain from his face. Eyes of deepest night stared at him. Sparks, small worms of fire, moved in those eyes. Evil thoughts and plans crawled through them even as Joel stared into their depths. The head turned back toward Thumbor.

Thumbor said, "I'm on Dragonel's business, bat. Leave me alone and get out of here."

The bat's voice was ice itself. "This cave is mine. No one tells me what to do here. And only the Queen is my mistress. Tell me your business, troll."

"My business is none of yours. Fly away, little bat, before I clip your wings." Thumbor reached for his axe.

"Dark words, troll. Ss–s–s–s–s–s." The bat hung heavily in the air.

"Go away. I don't like your talk. All I want is my supper and my peace." Thumbor's voice was loud and angry. He held his axe ready.

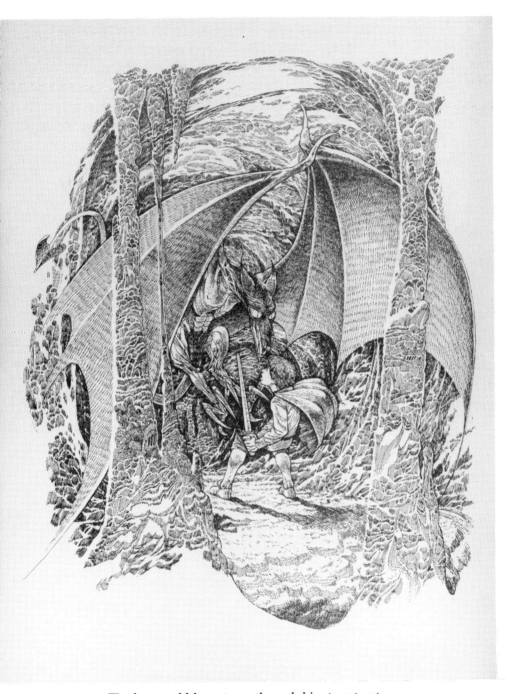

*The bat would have to go through him to get out.*

"Tss–s–s–s. Never has a troll spoken to me so boldly. Are you brave? I think not. You want to fight because you fear something else more than you fear me. The Witch Queen? Why so desperate, troll? Or are you a troll? I wonder? Sss–s–s–s–s. I'll find out, but not now."

The bat's wings began to move more quickly. It was going to leave. The plan had failed. It could return with terrible helpers. As the bat turned, Thumbor rose to his feet. Joel jumped up. He had to act. He took three quick steps. They carried him to the exact center of the passageway. There he stood. The bat would have to go through him to get out. It tried.

Joel gripped his sword with both hands. The bat checked in the air. It looked at him for a moment. A terrible smile twisted its mouth. It came at him with claws outstretched. From what Thumbor had told him, Joel knew that only the fangs carried poison. He waited as the claws drove at his side. He waited even as their sharp points bit into him. He waited while leather wings beat at him. He waited until the fangs came slashing down toward his throat. Then he stabbed upwards. The sword struck something and he drove it deeper. A thin, gurgling scream tore at his ears. Something hit him, smashed him to the ground. He knew nothing more.

# IX

## Bramble

Thumbor was leaning over him. Worry clouded the big man's eyes. "Joel, Joel, did it bite you? Joel?"

Joel shook his head and was sorry that he had. Red pain misted his eyes. He held his face in his hands.

"Your head? You were hit square by one of its wings. I think you'll only have a lump and headache, though. Your side will pain you some, too. But no bites. No bites. Thanks to all the powers for that! You live in luck, boy. You live in luck!"

Joel didn't feel very lucky. "My head **hurts!**"

Thumbor wiped Joel's forehead with a cold cloth. "It should," he growled, "And I hope it hurts for quite a while. You're a young fool. The only thing worse than that is an old fool like me."

Joel was confused. "What? Did the, the . . ."

"No, Joel. It's dead. It's deader than last year's weeds." Thumbor's face was deeply lined.

"Why?" Tears started to come. "Why are you . . . you angry . . ."

Thumbor took Joel's hand and held it tightly. Joel looked into his eyes. He said, "Joel, believe me, I'm not angry. You did a fine thing, a brave thing. You stopped that beast from killing us both. If it had gotten away . . . I was going to throw my axe. You started fighting it before I could make my cast. I was frightened for you. You can't know how happy I am that you're not hurt far worse than you are. You took such a great chance—more than you know." He smiled and squeezed Joel's hand again.

Joel let his eyes close. Relief and gladness filled him with a warmth that was proof against even the chill of that dank cave.

Thumbor said, "Here, drink this." Joel opened his eyes as a warm cup touched his lips. He drank, tasted sweet herbs and cinnamon. Thumbor said, "This will make you sleep. Your wounds aren't bad, but we must travel soon. A whole day's rest should make you near to being well." Thumbor smiled again. Joel fixed the smile in his mind and used it for an anchor as he drifted down into soft seas of sleep.

He awoke and found himself looking into yellow eyes. He blinked. It was the fox.

"I'm Bramble," the fox said. His very pointed nose was resting lightly on his shiny, black forepaws.

Joel said, "I . . . I'm Joel Burnham."

Bramble said, "I know. Your large friend has told me a great deal about you. He thinks quite highly of you, you know."

Joel, more than a little embarrassed, nodded.

The fox continued, "He also told me about your present adventure. I must admit that I am interested. I was on a quest of my own when I bumbled into that trap." He paused and rose gracefully to his feet. "You saved me. I owe you my life."

Joel said, "You owe us nothing. It was only right that we should help you."

The fox smiled sharply, "Still, I would like to help you in return. I would like to join your adventure. My nose and my wits could be of some use to you. Also, I might discover some bit of information which will help me in my own search."

Joel said, "What is your search?"

Bramble laughed, "It would take an hour and a week to tell the tale. Briefly, I'm looking for a lost friend. My friend has traveled into sorrow. I would bring him back."

Joel said, "Will you tell me your story?"

"I will," said Bramble, "but later. Again, will you let me join you? Thumbor has said that the decision is yours."

Joel paused. Thumbor had once more placed trust in his hands. The fox could help them. But would he remain true? Joel quickly saw that there could be no answer to this question. He and Thumbor could only hope. He said, "I want you to join us, Bramble." Joel held out his hand. Bramble raised his right forepaw and lightly touched Joel's outstretched fingers. Without words a promise had been made.

Joel raised himself from his blankets. He saw Thumbor kneeling close to a fire. His friend was cooking something in a stewpot. Joel got to his feet. His head felt fine (except for the lump by his ear) and his side gave him only a slight pinch. It was tightly bandaged. Joel and Bramble walked over to the fire.

Thumbor turned, "Ah, you've risen. How do you feel?"

Joel said, "Shaky and hungry."

Thumbor said, "It's no wonder. You've slept a day, a night, and most of another day. Does your side bother you?"

"No, not much. It sort of pinches."

Thumbor said, "It should be alright. The wound is clean and not too deep. It will itch like mad in a few days." He stirred the soup. "I see you two have met."

Joel said, "Yes, Thumbor, and I've asked Bramble to come with us. We can help each other." Joel shivered and looked at the place where the fire-bat had fallen. "We will need the help of friends if I'm not mistaken."

Thumbor said, "That is my thinking, too." He laughed, "Come, companion, eat some of my soup. We still have far to go. And we've stayed here too long!"

Bramble said, "No pepper for me, please."

They fell to eating.

Soon, they were ready to leave the fire-bat's cave. Joel learned from Bramble that the evil creature had not died quickly. Thumbor had finished it off with his axe. Later, he had thrown the broken body into the dark lake. The

73

cold, lapping waters were now dangerously poisonous. To taste of those waters would mean death to the drinker; only years of rains would clean the lake.

They left the cave at dusk. It was like coming out of prison. Joel felt that he had been underground for years instead of days. None of them were at all sorry to see the last of the toothless mouth of the cavern.

They traveled quickly and secretively. Bramble's keen nose and sharp hearing helped them avoid the few animals which made the desert their home. On their fifth night of travel they came to a river. Its water was muddy and smelled of sulphur. Bramble wrinkled his nose. Thumbor rubbed his chin. Joel looked from one to the other. He said, "Are we going to cross it?"

Thumbor said, "No, no. It's the river which flows down from Dragonel's castle. Over there, on the other side, is the road which leads to his front door. We don't want to go a-knocking. Not yet. We'll turn into the hills here and find a place from where we can watch. Be sharp, both of you. His guards are many and cruel." They turned from the foul river and began to climb.

Sunrise found them on a low hill beneath twisted pine trees. They looked out over a dead valley. Fire-blasted tree stumps and scorched rocks were everywhere. The murky river wound between grey humps of mud.

At the head of the valley, with its back to a mountain, stood a castle. Its stones were the color of lead. Battlements stuck up like broken teeth. Three toadstool towers stood above the walls. In the center of the largest tower was an iron gate. High above, on the tip of the mountain, stood a fourth tower. It was a black needle stabbing into dawn. Joel shook his head.

Thumbor said, "That is Dragonel's castle, Toadhorn. The Princess Meerlyn is almost certainly somewhere in that castle. We will try to find her tonight."

Joel said nothing. Bramble said, "My large friend, have you any sort of a plan? Are we to simply walk up and demand to be taken to the Princess? It's possible that the guards might object."

Thumbor laughed, "Yes, I have a very rough plan. You must help polish it."

Joel said, "What is it?" He had a feeling that he wasn't going to like what he was about to hear.

Thumbor began, "First of all, the Witch Queen is said to be away in the West. My fisherfolk friends have told me that she consorts with the wizards of the islands every year at this time. If she were here we would have no chance at all. Dragonel, the giant, is now in charge. We cannot fight him, but we might be able to fool him. I must become, once again, a troll. It will be my job to keep the giant busy. I will laugh with him, eat with him, drink with him. I will give him all the news of the forest while you two search the castle. There are only a few servants in the inner halls. All of the goblin-guards remain near the walls."

Bramble said, "That sounds simple enough. I suppose that we will hide in your bag and that you will carry us inside."

Thumbor said, "Yes, yes. There is a tricky bit, though."

Bramble smiled, "I'm used to finding flies in my honey."

Joel said, "What is the tricky part, Thumbor?"

Thumbor didn't smile. He said, "The fortress is divided into two parts. In the outer part live the guards, servants, and workers. The inner part is for Dragonel alone. Its only entrance is through the main dining hall. The door is right behind Dragonel's chair." Bramble looked at Joel. Joel looked back. "I will carry you in my bag. I'll put you down beneath the banquet table. You will have to make you own way from there."

Bramble said, "You talk as if you've been there before."

Thumbor smiled, "I have. Once there was a great gathering of trolls. I've seen the door, but I've never been through it."

Bramble said, "That should be a good tale. Let's hear it, Thumbor! We have all day."

Thumbor grinned, "Well, since you insist."

Joel said dryly, "Yes, aside from entertaining us, you might tell us something we need to know. We still haven't heard how we are to get away."

Thumbor smiled, "Well said, Joel." He cleared his throat, "Now, this is what happened. One night—more than ten years ago—I was tending my campfire far away in the South. Suddenly, I was no longer alone. A small, grey bat was sitting on a rock near the edge of my fire's glow. We exchanged such pleasantries as are common to creatures of the night. I offered it food and we talked.

"It said much that was unimportant. Bats aren't very bright, you know. Finally, though, it said something which made me sit up straight. It asked me when I was going to the big meeting. I pretended to know what it was talking about and said that I was leaving soon. It told me that was a wise thing to do. Dragonel, after all, had called the meeting and would roast anyone who was late.

"Eventually, the bat flew off into the darkness. I decided at once to go to this meeting. I knew that Dragonel was the leader of all trolls. I also knew that he had never gathered them all together in one place before. This sounded important.

"I traveled swiftly and at night. Twenty nights passed before I neared these lands. I knew that the grand meeting would be held at Toadhorn.

"On the twenty-first night I fell in with a band of true trolls. They, of course, thought I was one of them. They were an ugly bunch, but were friendly enough to me. It was with them that I passed through the iron gates of Toadhorn.

"We were the last to arrive. We were shown to a great hall. In that hall were more than two hundred trolls. Each one was uglier than a wart and as fierce as could be. It was a sight to frighten the strongest of men!

"Well, we all roared and laughed and carried on, as trolls will, until the huge door at the hall's farthest end crashed open. There stood Dragonel. Silence blew over us like a cold wind. He glared. His eyes were cold and blue. His red beard bristled. Every troll in that room shivered and looked down. Then, Dragonel laughed. No one else dared to join him.

"He told us all to sit down at his vast table. We did. And feasted on a great meal. Huge tanks of wine were drained that night, friends, believe me.

"When it was over he told us why we were there. He had planned a raid. He wanted all of the trolls to help him attack Gellnor (that's a city you haven't heard of, Joel) and carry off its riches. We were to storm through the night and knock down the gate with a great ram. After he told us this, he drank a toast to victory. The trolls cheered. And then, at midnight, he left. I haven't seen him since.

"At sunset the next day, I departed with the other trolls. Needless to say, I soon slipped away. I went straight to the king and told him what was about to happen. He summoned the army and planned a good welcome for those unwanted guests. It was an unpleasant surprise for my recent companions. Gellnor remained safe and there were, after that summer night, far fewer trolls in Tananar." Thumbor folded his hands.

Bramble said, "That was a most useful visit, my friend. I've heard of the troll-slaughter at Gellnor. I've wondered just how it was arranged. Now, I know. Well done!"

Joel smiled, "It was a good story, but it didn't make me feel any better about sneaking around inside of Toadhorn."

Thumbor grinned, "It's a pity that I didn't see more of the castle than I did. Such knowledge would help us greatly now!"

Bramble laughed, "Tut, tut, Thumbor. We'll manage. We'll tear old Toadhorn down stone by stone around Dragonel's ears if we must. We'll find Meerlyn."

Joel said, "Still, do you have any idea where in the castle Meerlyn might be?"

Thumbor said, "I'm not sure. Dragonel may have her in his rooms. She could be in the dungeon. And . . . she could be in the Witch's tower."

Joel looked at the midnight needle upon the mountain's crown. "That?"

Thumbor said, "Yes. You can see the stairs which lead to it. Look closely."

Joel did. Cut into the face of the cliff was a narrow stairway. It was almost impossibly steep. And it had no guard rails.

Thumbor continued, "Look there only if you have found her nowhere else. The Witch Queen has surely provided nasty surprises for those who would try to see her secret place."

Bramble eyed the faraway stairs, "Have no fear! We will stay off of that path if we can."

Thumbor said, "I'll keep watch in the great hall and await your return. That is where guests sleep. Dragonel will go to his rooms no sooner than midnight—and no later. Be done with your work before then. Any questions?"

Both Joel and Bramble were silent. There was nothing to ask.

Thumbor grinned, "Courage, friends. At dusk we'll enter Toadhorn castle. Let us rest now." They settled back beneath the trees and tried to sleep.

# X

## Dragonel

There was a heavy bump. Joel felt a sharp pain as his foot twisted beneath Bramble's claws. He grunted, "Ouch! Move over, Bramble."

Bramble hissed, "Move that sword of yours then. It's making holes in my ribs!"

"Quiet in there!" said Thumbor. "Do you want to be some goblin's supper?" Sitting inside of a bag with an unhappy fox can be most uncomfortable. It was hot and stuffy. They couldn't tell where they were, or what was happening.

All of their food and most of their equipment lay buried in the hill behind them. Thumbor hoped to claim it again after their escape from the castle.

The big man said, "Shhhh! We're going in now." Then Thumbor shouted, "Ho, the guard!"

An answering shout came from far above, "Who seeks to enter Toadhorn?"

Thumbor growled, "A troll, you frog's whelp! Let me in!"

Silence answered him. Several tense moments passed. Then a goblin's voice spoke from behind a barred spy-hole in the gate, "You, stand in the light of the torch so I can see you." Thumbor stepped beneath the torch. "Well, what do you want, troll?" demanded the goblin.

Thumbor said, "I want to see Dragonel. I've traveled to the very gates of Marl and have much news to tell our master."

"Enter," said the goblin. Joel heard the clang of the iron gate opening. Then there was the slap of leather boot-soles against stone. Minutes passed as they swayed with Thumbor's steps. Doors opened. Doors shut behind them. Finally, Thumbor stopped.

A voice like falling mountains said, "Welcome, troll. Your name is . . . . ?"

"Thumbor, master. My name is Thumbor." Joel and Bramble were tossed together as Thumbor bowed to the voice.

"Well, troll Thumbor, sit and eat. I wish news of the East. But first we will break our fast. Bogo, bring food and wine. Quickly, quickly, or I'll roast your toes for dessert!" There was the sound of running footsteps. "Now, troll Thumbor, sit."

Joel and Bramble felt themselves placed carefully on the floor. They waited. They heard Bogo return with roasted meat and wine. After a few moments they heard his footsteps retreat. Dragonel told Thumbor to eat. Noisily the giant and his guest both began to chew.

Slowly, carefully, Joel untied the cord fastening the pack. He made a small opening. Bramble then pushed the tip of his black nose out into the air. He sniffed. Only Thumbor and the giant were near. Quicker than an eye-blink he was out of the pack and crouching on the floor behind it. He looked around. No one watched. With a light scratch he signalled Joel. Soon, both were huddled against a tree-like table leg.

Joel could hardly believe what he saw. They were beneath the table. What a table! It was more like a house. Its bottom was yards above his head. He could see Thumbor's feet dangling in the air near him. The big man was sitting in a high-chair just like a small child.

Bramble motioned with his head. They moved warily along the length of the giant table. They tip-toed more quietly than any mice. Joel stared at the two boots planted at the table's end. Each boot was larger than a bathtub.

Bramble whispered, "Wait until he laughs. Then we'll dodge between his feet and right under his chair. From there it will be easy."

Joel nodded. At that moment they heard a roar from overhead. Bramble was already beneath the chair. Joel scrambled after him. The giant raised his foot. Joel dove as a swimmer would dive into a lake. The huge boot missed him by inches. He tumbled painfully to the floor. The giant hadn't heard.

Bramble flashed across the floorboards. He turned and crouched in the shadow of the great door. Joel swallowed hard. Ten yards of open space lay between him and that door. He waited. Bramble's eyes bored into his. Hurry. Hurry. He closed his eyes. Fear was cold inside him. He wished for some magic to carry him through danger. There was none. Lor was cold against his chest. He would have to find magic in himself.

He held his sword tightly against his side and began to run. His feet felt heavy. His heart was a stone in his chest. The giant's back rose above him like a cliff. The head began to turn. Joel slipped into shadow, darkness.

They lay trembling for several minutes. They were just out of sight in a short hallway. Slowly they rose to their feet and walked to the door. Joel pushed against its rough boards. It didn't move. He looked at Bramble. Bramble looked upwards at the iron latch. It was far above their heads. Bramble looked back at Joel. He didn't need to say anything.

Joel never could remember how he made that climb. With fingers and toes jammed into the large cracks between timbers, he rested. His arms hurt. Below, Bramble waited.

He reached out and pulled down on the door latch. It moved quietly and easily. Silently the door swung inwards. Joel climbed quickly down. He leaped the last six feet and nearly landed on Bramble. He got to his feet and turned.

A large room lay before them. Red flames from torches did little more than make shadows. They could dimly see two stairways. One led up into smoky darkness. The other led down.

Bramble whispered, "We may as well start at the bottom of this place. They may have put her in the dungeon."

Joel nodded.

The steps descending to the dungeon were huge blocks of black stone. They were damp and slippery. Torches burned in braces on the walls, but their light was swallowed by the dank air. Breathings of mould and slime flowed around them. Hints of darker smells rose from below. They climbed carefully from stone to stone.

After one hundred steps they reached a room. In this room were tools—knives, spikes, hammers, chains. There were tables and benches. There were racks. These things had been used to hurt people. Fear lay over them like dust.

Bramble said, "This is Dragonel's special place."

Joel forced himself to speak, "Where, where would she be?"

Bramble said, "Over there. That must be the cell. There probably is only one. People who are brought here are brought here alone."

Alone. Joel looked once at the scorched, stained boards of a table. He understood a new meaning of that word.

They walked across the room. A door of iron bars finally halted them. They looked between the bars into darkness. Nothing moved. They could see nothing. Joel climbed upon a bench. He pulled a torch from its brace. He hopped down. The cold touch of the wood made him wish for sunlight. He thrust the torch between the bars. Red light filled the cell. In a corner lay a heap of bones and the ragged remnants of a king's guard's uniform. But there was no sign of Meerlyn.

Grimly they hurried back to the stairway. As fast as they could they climbed away from that room of pain. They stopped when they reached the top of the stairway.

Bramble laughed a silent, fox-laugh. His teeth shone. Joel looked at him wonderingly. The fox said, "I'll bet we're the first visitors ever to have walked back up those stairs." He looked at Joel. Joel thought of the unfortunate guard and nodded. They turned to the other stairway and climbed the giant steps.

Soon they found themselves in a long hallway. At its far end were two doors. They began to walk as quickly as they dared. Grim axes hung from the walls. They reminded Joel that every step carried him farther from any hope of safety. The stairs behind him would soon echo with the footfalls of the giant.

They reached the end of the hall. The door on the left was iron. The one on the right was made of wood. Either was large enough for a barn, sturdy enough for a fortress.

Joel put his shoulder against the wooden door. It had no latch. Slowly it began to move. He braced his feet against the floor and pushed harder. He was at last able to open a crack just wide enough for them to slip through. Inside were the giant's rooms.

Joel rubbed his shoulder and looked around. With a small shock he recognized familiar things grown terribly large. What he had at first taken to be a building of some sort was a bed. Vast chairs and a table were pushed against a far wall. A spiked club the size of a small oak tree leaned against an oversized chest of drawers. On the near wall hung a mirror the size of a pond.

Bramble stood still and sniffed the air. He raised his left forepaw and arched his neck. He turned to face the chest of drawers. He lowered his head. "I can't tell. Some human has been here recently. It's possible that someone is still here."

Joel said, "Where?"

"Over there. On top of that great, wooden thing."

Joel frowned, "Well, it looks as if I'll have to do some more climbing."

The fox said nothing, but smiled toothily.

Joel said, "Wait here, near the door. Bark softly if you hear the giant coming."

Joel crossed the wide floor quickly. He was glad when he reached the shadow of the chest. He looked at the boards which made up its back. They were rough—ridged and cracked. Climbing would be tiring, but simple. He began.

Many minutes later he rested his elbows on the top of the chest. With a grunt he kicked his way completely up. He lay panting for several moments. Finally, he rose to his feet.

Far away, across the room, he could see Bramble anxiously pacing by the door. He turned. Several large, dark objects rested on the top of the chest. He walked towards the nearest. It was a box. He hoisted himself over its edge and saw gold—several pieces of outsized jewelry. He let himself down. The next object was as large as a coach. It was covered with a fine, silken cloth. Joel gently drew back its folds.

A soft voice said, "Who comes unasked to the nest of the giant?"

Joel stood stone still.

# XI

## The Singing Cage

Again, the voice said, "Who's there? Be not afraid, stranger. I am an enemy of the giant. Talk to me. I long to hear the voice of a friend."

Joel felt his blood begin to unfreeze. He said, "How do you know that I'm your friend?"

The voice said, "Well, you are here, and you are not a captive."

Joel lifted the cloth again. "Where are you?"

There was silvery laughter and the voice said, "I'm here, in front of you, above you. I am the Singing Cage. My name is Rhiannon." Joel stood silent in wonder. He didn't know what to say.

Rhiannon went on, "I was made by mages of the Eastern Sea, from gold not now found in this world. Will you hear my story, boy? I see now that that is what you are."

Joel said, "I'll listen, but hurry! Dragonel . . ."

Rhiannon said, "A moment only. I protected the young of the great sea-birds. Their feathers are as green as the backs of waves at dawn. Their spirits are cloud-free. But, if given the sky, the small ones would fly until death claimed them. I sheltered them while they became strong. I taught them the songs of their people. I served them well for long years. Then, the Witch Queen came in a smoky fog. She killed the young birds and took me. She took me from my home over the sea and brought me here. She gave me as a gift to Dragonel. Against my will I've served his dark ends. Only a change in the world, or death, will bring me freedom. Oh how I await the fall of Toadhorn castle! The chains holding me are strong."

Joel was quiet. He needed something to say. He spoke at last, "Have you waited here long?"

"Yes, boy, many times your years I've sat in this room.

Your voice is young, very young. How came you here? And why?"

Joel stammered, "I . . . I'm . . . . My name is Joel. I am seeking a captive of the Witch Queen."

Rhiannon said, "I thought as much. You are seeking Princess Meerlyn. I know her well. She has brightened many hours for me. I hope that you can reach her. Would that I could help you more! I can only tell you where she is."

"That alone would be very great help!" said Joel.

"Alas," said Rhiannon, "You know of the high tower?"

"Yes."

"It is there that she is being held."

Joel never knew before that words could be cold, but Rhiannon's sad report sank like an icicle into his heart. He said, "We must help her."

Rhiannon said, "It will be dangerous to go to her. You know that already. I know of one of the dangers. Beware of the steps. Test each one with a staff. Some are made only of air."

Joel said, "I will go now. You have my thanks. I wish I could help you."

Rhiannon said, "Joel, you can. You are not alone, are you?"

"I have friends with me," Joel admitted.

"One of your friends is Telmeer, correct?"

"Yes, but he is far away."

"I thought as much. He is a friend of mine, too. He knows I am here. Wish him well for me, please."

"I will. Can," Joel paused, "can he help you?"

"He has been trying to help since the day of my capture."

Joel looked down. "Now," Rhiannon said, "good-bye, good fortune, and may silence go with you!"

"Good-bye!" Joel turned and walked to the back of the chest. He started to lower himself over the edge. Suddenly, he heard Bramble's high bark. He jerked his eyes toward the door. The fox was already halfway across the room streaking for the shadow of the giant's bed. Joel straightened up. He looked from side to side. Where could he go?

"Hissssst!" The voice was Rhiannon's. "Joel, to me. Come to me!"

Joel turned and ran across the rough boards. He stumbled into the side of the cage. Breathless, he said, "Where?"

Rhiannon spoke softly, "Behind and beneath the cover. Do not dare to look. Dragonel's eyes have a power which few can fight. If you look into them, you will run screaming to his hand. Breathe small breaths and cover your eyes. Quickly!"

Joel did as she said. He crouched close to the wood and trembled. He heard footsteps. They were not what he had expected. They didn't crash and make the floor quake. They were soft, but powerful, like the distant booming of a great drum. They came closer. Joel felt a swish of air as the door opened. The footsteps crossed the room. Huge hands gripped the chest. Joel's heart pounded within him. Wood grated as a drawer was pulled open. Joel could hear the steamy hiss of Dragonel's breath. The chest trembled. Large things were being thrown about in the drawer. There was a deep, cave-grunt of satisfaction. The drawer was closed. The footsteps retreated. The door closed. Silence fell like a cloud.

**Minutes passed.** At last, Rhiannon said, "Make haste, Joel. He will not return for awhile. Go through the iron door and straight down the hall of dark mirrors. The last door opens upon your path. Remember to test each step. Farewell!"

Joel stood. He had not seen Rhiannon unveiled. Perhaps he never would. Sudden, surprising sadness at this parting washed away the last of his fear. He said, "Goodbye again. I will give Telmeer your greeting and ask him to send you comfort—if he can. Someday, I'll try to come **back . . . good-bye." He turned and ran back to the edge** of the chest.

Quickly, he lowered himself to the floor. Bramble was waiting for him. Worry burned yellow in the fox's eyes. Without words they crossed to the door. Joel put his shoulder to its splintered boards. It stuck for a second and then moved easily. They slipped through the crack and ran across the hall to the shadow of the iron door.

Joel looked up. A bar of steel held the door shut. He began to climb. He reached the steel bar just before his arms gave out. He had to rest for several moments. He caught his breath and looked at the bar. It was pushed into a hole deep in the square posts which framed the door. It would have to be pulled out of that hole before the door would move. Joel put his back against the wood and braced his feet against a steel cross-piece. He pushed with all of his strength. Nothing happened. He pushed again until his muscles began to tear. Slowly, the bar moved. Joel heaved again. The bar slid out of the hole with a clang and the door swung open. Grabbing the cross-piece, he just saved himself from a bad fall. He managed to reach the cracked wood of the door-post. Shaking, he climbed down.

They hurried through the black gap between the door and the post. Gloom surrounded them. Only distant moonlight touched the upper reaches of a long hall. They turned back to the door and pulled it as far shut as they could. They could only hope that Dragonel wouldn't discover that it had been opened.

Joel slumped to the floor. He said, "I've got to rest!"

Bramble nearly said something sharp, but his words became soft as he spoke them, "You've worked mightily this night, Joel. Tell me, what happened in the giant's room?"

Joel told him of Rhiannon and finished saying, "We must test each step as we go and also watch for other traps."

Bramble said, "Are you ready?"

Joel said, "Yes . . . as ready as I'll ever be." They both smiled.

# XII

## The Silver Snake

They walked silently through the shadowy hall. Mirrors like dark pools of water hung on either wall. Moonlight gleamed strangely in their depths. At the hall's end was a pointed arch. Through it waited the night sky.

They passed beneath the arch and out into the open. Black stairs swept up in a curve to their right. Joel took out his sword. He probed the wide step in front of them. It was stone. He probed another. They began to climb.

Distance grew beneath them. Red torches held by goblin hands were sparks on the walls far below. Joel thrust at another step. His sword slid deep into the seeming stone. He jumped back.

Bramble said quietly, "A false one?"

"Yes." Joel wiped sweat from his eyes. "Yes."

The fox backed to the edge of the step upon which they were standing. "I'll make the leap. Wait until I've safely landed before you follow."

Joel spoke sharply, "No! Wait! What if the next step is false, too?"

Bramble grinned without humor and said, "Then you'll know not to trust it, my boy." The fox gathered himself, took three quick steps and jumped. His body arched high in the air. The stairs were wide, but he came down squarely in the middle of the one above the gap. It was stone. He turned and said, "Sheath your sword, Joel. Jump high and throw yourself forward."

Joel readied himself. He looked down. The boiling river seemed no larger than a thin wire of tin. The giant walls and towers of Toadhorn itself seemed like the toys of some evil child. Joel swallowed hard and crouched. He jumped outwards and up. His right foot landed on stone. His left foot grazed stone and slide into air. He threw his body foward. Both of his feet were hanging over the drop. He began to slide backwards. He felt Bramble's teeth fasten on his sleeve. He saw the fox's muscles tighten with strain. He slowed, stopped, but for a moment only. Bramble's claws scraped over smooth stone. They both began to slide into the endless night below.

Then the buckle of Joel's swordbelt caught on the stair's edge, caught and held. He stopped. His fingers found a small ridge of rock. Bramble gave a mighty heave and Joel swung one leg over the edge. He rolled and was safe in the middle of the stair. He lay panting for several minutes. Finally, he raised his head, looked at Bramble, and said, "Thanks, friend."

Bramble stopped licking his paw. Without smiling he said, "You are terribly clumsy."

Joel nearly strangled with silent laughter. With his eyes the fox smiled a small, dry smile.

They found two more steps of air, each smaller than the first and easier to leap. They should have been tired when they reached the top of the stairway. They weren't. Instead cold, quiet dread filled their minds and drowned out the cries of tired muscles. Above them reached the black needle of the Witch Queen's tower.

They crossed bare rock to stand before a tunnel leading into the tower, a dark mouth. They looked at each other. Silently, Bramble stepped into the entrance. Joel followed.

They walked slowly foward. Damp, thick air flowed around them like the waters of some underground river. They could barely see their way. They came to a corner, turned it, and found themselves in a wide chamber. Three torches burned smokily on the far wall. In that wall was a door of deepest, midnight black. Its handle gleamed silver in the red light. They walked toward it trying to look in all directions at once. Nothing seemed dangerous. Nothing seemed to threaten.

*As the blade slid free, the snake came to life.*

They came to within a few feet of the door. Bramble was still leading. Joel reached out to grasp the handle. He looked at it. Then slowly he pulled his hand back. He stared at the handle. It was a silver, shining snake. Thumbor's tale flashed in his mind. He put his hand to his sword. Bramble looked at him curiously. Joel pulled the sword from its sheath. As the blade slid free, the snake came to life.

It struck with the speed of a flame. Bramble twisted nearly in half and rolled to his left. Silver fangs missed his throat by a breath. Joel swung his sword with both hands. It passed through the snake's tail and crashed in sparks against rock. The wounded snake reared, its fangs bared. Joel's hands were inches from the open mouth. Bramble leaped. His teeth closed on the snake's neck just behind its head. There was a wild hissing sound and then silence.

Bramble kept his death-hold for a minute more. Then, he jumped backwards and away. Joel stepped forward with his sword raised, but the snake was dead. Green poison seeped from its fangs and stained the dark stones. As the two watched, its torn body turned again to hard metal.

Joel said, "Thumbor told me of this thing. He made it. It was the Witch Queen's toy."

"More likely," said Bramble, "it was her tower's guardian. A good one, too. Either of us could have died here."

Joel shivered as he looked at the silver coils on the floor. He said, "We'd better go on. The night is getting old and we'll need darkness for our escape."

Bramble murmured, "That's not all we'll need."

They opened the door and went through it. Stairs rose up into the tower in ever tightening circles. Testing the stairs again, they began climbing. They came at length to a trapdoor directly overhead. They looked carefully for anything which might hint of an ambush. They found nothing. Joel pushed up on the door and was startled by a squealing scream. He again drew his sword. Bramble flashed over the lip of the opening. Joel was close behind him.

They found themselves in a circular room. Through a great square gap in the roof they saw a bat-shape disappearing. Out of the night's darkness came its echoing screech. Bramble's eyes glowed yellow. "That's trouble, Joel! The Witch Queen's pet is off to warn her. That's trouble!"

Joel said, "We can't help it. We can only hurry." With that he lowered his eyes and looked around the room. There was no sign of Meerlyn. Only strange shapes greeted his inspection. They walked slowly through and around the Witch Queen's unnameable tools. The dark instruments were still, but theirs was the promised threat of their mistress's coming. Of the Princess Meerlyn they found no sign.

Bramble stopped dead. He sniffed musty air. He listened. "She is here. There is a trick to this. Touch the wall over there, Joel. Something is not right about it."

Joel moved close to the wall. He pressed one of its stones. Nothing happened. The stone seemed solid. He moved a few feet to his right and pressed another stone. It moved, but only a tiny fraction of an inch.

Bramble, watching closely, said, "What is it?"

Joel said, "It moved, but strangely. For a second it seemed as if the stone was something soft. Then it seemed to freeze."

Bramble said, "Use your sword. Push it slowly into the base of the wall. Don't push it in more than a few inches. Slowly cut out the shape of a door."

Joel said, "I can't cut through stone!"

Bramble said, "Try. There is magic in this. Be careful, though, someone may be behind that wall."

Joel shrugged his shoulders and knelt on the floor. He placed the tip of his sword against the wall and pushed.

He nearly fell over with surprise. The blade went in smoothly. The wall cut like butter. Quickly he made the shape of a door. He pulled his sword easily out of the seeming stone and returned it to its scabbard. He needed no further prompting from Bramble. Reaching up he pulled at the edge of the cut he'd made. Gray stone instantly became gray silk. Fine cloth floated down over his hand. The wall was really only an enchanted curtain. On its far side stood a girl.

She was tall, taller than Joel by a few inches. Her hair was dark and her eyes were deep and calm. She stood very still.

Bramble stepped forward, "My lady, Princess Meerlyn?"

She spoke, "Yes. Who are you?"

Bramble said, "I am Bramble and this is Joel Burnham."

Meerlyn's eyes rested briefly on the fox and then turned toward Joel. Joel felt as if he were standing before a stern judge. He met her sharp, queenly gaze without flinching.

"We have come far and dared much to find you," Bramble said. "We hope to help you return to your father, your home."

She said, "A noble hope. A kind purpose. But do you speak truly? The Queen of this evil realm has tried to trick me before. She would use me in her plans. How can you prove that you mean well, that you are friends?"

Bramble looked at Joel. Joel said, "We are friends of Thumbor. He is waiting for us down below."

"Thumbor? Thumbor is here?"

"Yes!" Joel smiled, "He told me how you rescued him that night at Tullyman."

Meerlyn's eyes were bright, "That is good news! It is nearly proof enough that you are who you say you are. However, it could be more of the Witch's cleverness. She could know about Thumbor and me." Meerlyn paused. After a moment she said,

"In seas of fear
With darkness near
Your strength is sand—"

Then Joel looked into her eyes and said,

"Only courage stands—
And one thing more—
A star's bright heart—Lor."

He took the leather pouch from around his neck. He untied the binding thongs and removed Lor from its protecting cover. The jewel blazed, filling the room with yellow light.

Meerlyn's eyes shone golden brown. She said, "You have proved yourselves. I will come with you, thankfully. Thankfully. My heart is too full." She smiled and there was more light in that light-killing room.

Bramble said, "Haste, haste! News of our presence here is speeding to Dragonel and the Witch Queen as we talk. They will be after us. Down the stairs and quickly!"

Joel bound the jewel in its pouch and put it beneath his shirt. Bramble led the way through the trapdoor. Joel and Meerlyn turned to follow him. Together they climbed down and left that dark room forever.

# XIII

## Escape

They hurried down the spiral stairs. At the door Meerlyn's eyes widened. The coils of the silver snake still lay upon the floor of the entrance chamber. They all kept well clear of it, but they didn't pause.

At the top of the outer stairs, they found that the moon had set. Deepest night wrapped itself close about them. They fairly ran down the stairs of stone, mindless of the depths to their left.

Soon, Bramble said, "Slowly, slowly. Stop!"

Then, Joel remembered! The false stairs!

Bramble chuckled in the darkness, "Yes, my friend, I counted them. Test the stairs in front of me, if you please."

Joel took his sword from its scabbard. He thrust at the stair. It was solid. He stepped down. He thrust again. Nothingness. This one was air.

The leap through darkness into darkness was frightening, but this downward jump was much easier than any of those upward jumps they had made on their climb to the tower. They passed the other false stairs in safety.

Swiftly they entered and swept through the hall of shaded mirrors. They stopped when they reached the iron door.

Bramble said, "Wait, quiet." His ears pointed forwards sharply. His nose quivered. "I can't tell. I don't think that the giant awaits us, but I can't tell."

Joel said, "We can't fight him. Not for long, anyway."

Meerlyn said, "It would take forever to reach the courtyard by any other route. We must open the door."

Joel drew his sword and said, "I'll pull the door open and strike his foot if he's there."

Meerlyn said, "Pulling and striking are two very different actions. Give me the sword. I'll guard you." Joel looked at her doubtfully.

"Quickly," Bramble said, "give it to her. She's right and—if stories are true—she's also a dangerous fighter."

Joel handed Meerlyn the sword and grasped the door. He pulled. Muscles in his back strained. He pulled harder and the door began to move. The crack between it and its frame became just wide enough for them to slip through. Bramble streaked past his feet. Meerlyn squeezed by his shoulder. He followed her.

Dragonel was not waiting for them. The hallway was empty. Joel and Meerlyn both pulled on the door. They managed to get it nearly closed. Silently they turned and sped away from the sleeping giant's rooms.

Down the last giant stairway they leaped. It seemed to Joel like years since he and Bramble had climbed it. He and Meerlyn reached the door which opened upon the banquet hall. It was shut and latched. Joel rubbed his weary arms and frowned.

Meerlyn saw him and smiled—not without kindness. She moved close to the door, looked up, and began to climb. In a few moments she had undone the latch and dropped back down beside him. Together, they pulled the door open. Bramble came down the stairs (he had been keeping watch above) and joined them. They found Thumbor waiting in the darkened hall.

The big man smiled broadly as he went down on one knee in a deep bow to Meerlyn. Kneeling still, he grabbed Joel with his left arm and hugged him roughly. In his right hand he held his great axe. He lowered it, extended one finger and softly touched Bramble's back. They all grinned at each other in complete happiness.

Meerlyn came forward and put her hand on Thumbor's shoulder, "My thanks, old friend." She smiled, "My thanks to all of you."

Thumbor rose, "It's too soon to thank us, My Lady. We have yet to escape the castle. Come, we must hurry!"

Bramble said, "Thumbor, wait, you must know this. There was a messenger, a bat-guard. We couldn't stop it. The Witch Queen will soon know what has been done this night."

Thumbor frowned in thought. After several moments, he said, "You have been through much danger already. Now, we will all endure more. I had hoped that we could leave as we came. We can't. Dragonel will be upon us. There is another way out of this castle, a terrible way. We must take the chance that we can pass it in safety. Beyond it, I think, is a place where we can be hidden from the giant's vengeance. Come."

There was a scraping noise in a dark corner of the hall. Joel turned. Yellow goblin eyes stared out at him from the shadows. Thumbor seized him and shouted, "Bogo! Bogo, come here! Help me! I've caught these humans coming down the stairs. They're trying to escape."

Bogo blinked at Thumbor and then came shambling quickly across the hall. As he neared Meerlyn, the goblin's long hairy arms reached out to grasp her. Suddenly, Thumbor's hand shot out and closed around Bogo's skinny throat. The goblin's eyes bulged as Thumbor lifted him into the air. The big man calmly said, "Joel, get the rope out of my pack."

Joel ran to the green pack, opened it, lifted out the rope, and then ran back to Thumbor with the heavy coil. In a few moments Bogo was securely wrapped up. Thumbor finished tying the last knot and said, "Now, Joel, run and get a spare sock. Bogo will soon have enough breath back to yell for his master." Joel ran again to the pack, found a sock, and returned with it to Thumbor. Thumbor said, "Stuff it into his mouth, Joel. That should keep him quiet. I'll look around for a place where we can hide him." Joel nodded. Thumbor smiled, "Mind your fingers. Goblin teeth are sharp." The big man rose and walked over to the vast fireplace.

Joel glanced nervously toward the door which led to the upper part of the castle. Meerlyn stood watch there. At the other end of the hall, Bramble was poised, ears forward, listening for the approach of goblin guards.

A shattering howl split the air at his feet. Bogo! Bogo was trying to warn Dragonel! Joel's heart skipped two beats before he managed to kneel and push the woolen sock into Bogo's wide-open mouth. The siren-like howl immediately became a muffled grunt, but the damage was done.

Thumbor came striding around the corner of the giant's table. Joel looked up and said, "I'm sorry, Thumbor. I thought that he was still dazed."

Thumbor said, "There's no time for apologies. What's done is done. Dragonel will be here in minutes." He stooped and lifted Bogo as easily as a child might lift a mouse. "To the fireplace, Joel, hurry!" Joel scrambled to his feet and followed Thumbor.

Meerlyn reached the fireplace a step behind Joel. Her eyes were wide and dark. In a near whisper she said, "Dragonel comes. I heard him leave his room."

Thumbor motioned toward a huge black kettle which hung from an iron hook set into the stones of the hearth. "I'm going to put you all in there. Stay hidden until I come for you —or until Dragonel leaves." He smiled grimly, "And keep Bogo quiet!" Joel and Meerlyn both nodded. Quickly Thumbor dropped Bogo into the kettle. He turned and gently lifted Meerlyn. Bramble glided up just as she disappeared over the kettle's rough rim.

Bramble looked up at Thumbor and said, "Surely you're not planning to cook us?"

Thumbor grunted, "Dragonel's coming. Don't . . . "

A dull boom echoed through the hall. Another, like the distant fall of mountains, made the floor quiver.

Thumbor looked from Bramble to Joel. "He's on the stairs."

Joel held out his arms. In an instant the fox was resting lightly against his chest. Thumbor picked them both up and lifted them high. He let go and the black kettle swallowed them.

Joel landed on the kettle's curved bottom and nearly tripped over Meerlyn. She was sitting beside Bogo with her hands clamped over the goblin's mouth. Bramble leapt lightly to the iron floor. Joel sat down next to Meerlyn and helped her hold onto the squirming goblin.

Bramble, looking distastefully at the kettle's greasy walls, said, "It's a good thing that the fire is out. Still, we've done half of the giant's work for him. Here we are, sitting in his pot just waiting to be cooked."

Meerlyn said, "Shhhh! Dragonel is . . . "

A thundering crash rolled across the hall as Dragonel flung open the great door. Stones shivered and the kettle swung wildly back and forth on its iron hook.

"BOGO!" Dragonel roared. "BOGO! Where are you, you son of a rat? Come out and tell me why you've spoiled my sleep."

Thumbor rose to his feet. He had just managed to dive beneath his blanket before Dragonel had thrown open the door. He said, "Ma—Master, what do you wish?"

Dragonel glared at him. The red bristles of the giant's beard were standing straight out, "Are your ears made of stone, troll? Did you not hear my servant's scream? It came from here. Bogo could have been sitting on your chest!"

"Master," said Thumbor, "I heard something, but it was not close to here. It was higher, far up in the tower, I think."

Dragonel's eyes were dark slits in his face. The muscles in his huge arms knotted with suppressed rage. "Troll, you're lying to me. I'll hang you from the eastern wall and let the sun take you if you don't tell me at once what happened to Bogo. Have you killed him?"

"No, master, no! I swear! I've not seen Bogo since he served us at supper. I am a heavy sleeper, though. I could be mistaken about what I heard."

Dragonel took a step toward Thumbor. "Troll, something is not right about this. Something is hidden." He took another step toward Thumbor. "I will know the truth before I'm through with you."

Thumbor tensed his muscles, readied himself to dodge the giant. He had already decided to try for the stairs. Perhaps he could reach the mountaintop and lose himself in the darkness. Perhaps.

Suddenly, there was a clatter of iron-shod feet at the hall's far end. A dozen torch-bearing goblins burst into the room. Their leader—a stout, warty goblin in black armor—rushed forward and said, "Master, master, the bat-guard has flown down from the Queen's tower. An escape is taking place. Humans are on the high stairway."

Dragonel looked from Thumbor to the goblin captain. Then he turned his eyes back to Thumbor. "I might be wrong about you, troll. We'll see." He turned back to the goblin captain. "Up the stairs, lout!" he roared. "What are you waiting for?" The goblin captain cowered and then sprang foward, followed by his troops.

Dragonel looked at Thumbor once again. "You," he jabbed his finger at Thumbor, "guard this door. Don't move. We'll talk again—later."

Thumbor lowered his eyes and said, "Yes, master. Yes. I'll guard the door."

Dragonel glared at him once more and then turned to follow the goblin guards. Thumbor sighed, deeply and silently, with relief. He waited until he was sure that the giant had truly departed and then went over to the kettle. He said, "Meerlyn, hold up your hands. I'll lift you out." She did and she was soon standing by Thumbor. "Joel," he called, "hold Bramble up."

Bramble, as the big man lifted him gently out of Joel's

101

hands, said, "We've escaped the stew-pot this time, but we'll be in it again soon if we don't hurry."

Thumbor said, "I know, my friend. I know."

Thumbor put Bramble down and then helped Joel out of the kettle. When he had his feet on the floor, Joel said, "Thumbor, what shall we do with Bogo?"

Thumbor smiled, "Leave him in the pot, Joel. He'll be hidden in there and it will be morning before anyone discovers him."

"Yes," said Bramble, "and he'll be safe, too. Unless Dragonel decides to heat the pot, then he'll find himself with a mess of goblin soup."

Thumbor chuckled and said, "Enough, Bramble, enough. Come, we must leave this hall at once. Dragonel may return at any time. Step quietly and watch the doorways. There may be more guards." Thumbor turned and began walking.

They followed him past the huge table and out of the banquet hall. They moved silently through empty rooms. A few torches cast red light into shadows. There were no guards.

At last, they neared a small door. Thumbor motioned for them to stop. He turned and whispered, "Outside is the courtyard. We have to walk its length without being seen. Stay in the shadow of the wall. Be silent. Most of the goblin guards are on the battlements or charging up to the Witch Queen's tower, but we can't take chances."

Bramble stepped out of the door first. Thumbor followed him. Joel and Meerlyn went out together. Step by careful step they made their way along the wall. Joel felt that hours, not minutes, were passing. Across the courtyard, atop the battlements he could see helmets and spears against the stars.

A distant cry of terror suddenly tore the silence of the night. Joel looked up. What looked like a flaming red star was falling from high on the mountain stairway.

Bramble whispered, "A goblin torch . . . and a goblin, too, I don't doubt. Goblins never were very good at counting."

Joel shivered and tried not to think about how close he and Bramble had come to suffering the fallen goblin's fate. Thumbor motioned for them to hurry. They went on.

Long moments later they stopped. They had reached the end of the inner wall. A few yards ahead of them the outer wall curved in to meet the mountain. All was quiet.

Thumbor leaned close and whispered, "Postern gate. No guards. Cross one by one. I'll go last." They all nodded.

Bramble was a brief blur in the darkness. Joel readied himself, glanced at the battlements, and then ran. He was across the open space in a few steps. Still, his heart pounded after he reached the safety of the small gate. Meerlyn was beside him before he even turned to look back. Thumbor quickly joined them.

The big man easily lifted an iron bar which served as the gate's lock. Slowly he opened the gate. One by one, with Bramble leading, they walked into free air beyond Dragonel's walls.

Suddenly, they heard rolling thunder behind them. Joel realized it was the angry roar of Dragonel. They turned and fled into the night.

103

# XIV

## Tree of Knives

Thumbor led them along the base of the cliff. Stepping softly, they stayed in the shadows. When they were well out of sight of the battlements, he stopped.

"The next part is hard. Soon, we will come to a boiling stream. It joins the river below us. Above, it springs from between the roots of a tree. That tree is a monster. It guards the narrow pass which is our path to safety."

Bramble said, "I've heard something of this tree. It is said that no enemy of the Witch Queen passes it alive."

Thumbor nodded, "What you have heard is true."

Meerlyn said, "How are we to fool it then?"

Thumbor said, "I will become a troll again. I'll tell the tree that I'm on an errand for Dragonel. You and Joel will be my captives. Bramble, you will have the pleasure of another ride in my bag. There's no explaining you away. We need a disguise for Meerlyn, too. I had one for her in the gear we left behind. Now, Joel's hooded cloak will have to do." They bustled about, rearranging themselves as Thumbor instructed.

Bramble was not happy about riding in the bag. He said, "I'd rather be worn as a hat than be carried like a potato."

"Peace, friend!" said Thumbor. "This tree is the most dangerous creature we have yet faced. Its branches are covered with poisoned thorns that it flings against its enemies. It is evil, old and suspicious." They were silent.

Joel finally said, "Thumbor, how are we to act, Meerlyn and me?"

He looked at Joel and said, "I'm not sure what the rules of passage are. We will have to feel them out. You and Meerlyn must walk stiffly and not speak. Act as if some spell of obediance has been put on you. When we get to the tree, I will tell you to keep walking. I may give other orders. Obey them, but slowly. Meerlyn, you will go first and carry the bag. Joel, you follow her. Stay a few yards apart. I'll tell the tree that we must hurry. That's true enough, but it will sound true for other reasons as well. Trolls must never dare the light of the sun and it's nearly dawn."

A muffled voice came from the bag, "Well, let's get going. I might begin to sprout before you get through talking." They all laughed—quietly.

"One more thing," Thumbor's voice was serious again, "If I cry 'down' then make yourself one with the earth. It will mean that the tree is trying to kill us." The girl and the boy both nodded. They rose. The sky was getting lighter. They began to walk.

Soon, they came to the boiling stream. It hissed evilly over rocks. Foul-smelling steam rose into the air above it. They turned and climbed beside it.

Joel tried to make his steps stiff and lifeless. It wasn't hard to do. He was very tired. He tried not to look at that place ahead where the mountains came together. He looked at Meerlyn's back. She was plodding along, too.

It was strange, very strange. He had met her only a few hours before. He had spoken no more than a few words to her. He knew almost nothing about her, but she was his friend. Meerlyn, High Princess of Marl, a girl, was his friend. He could not doubt it. Something in his heart told him that it was true.

Also, he was very happy. He was dirty. He was more tired than he had thought he could ever be. He had been more frightened than he ever again wanted to be. His body had been scraped, banged, and painfully bruised. He hurt all over, but he was happy. For the first time he understood that never before had he known true friends. Thumbor, Bramble, Meerlyn—all would risk themselves to help him. And he would give all he had to help any of them.

Joel smiled to himself. He had not yet seen the magic of Lor. The jewel had thumped against his chest for many miles, but he had nearly forgotten about it. He wondered when it would be of use. Adventures, it seemed, were mostly very hard work and very little magic.

Meerlyn slowed. Joel looked up in spite of himself. The ground became level a short way ahead of them. Mountain walls came nearly together. Just below the narrowest part of the path stood a squat tree. It was far wider than it was tall. Its branches were thick and sinewy. It had few leaves, but many cruel thorns.

The monster tree heard them coming. With a windless swaying of limbs it twisted around to look at them. Red eyes glared out from between wrinkled folds of bark. Joel looked down.

Thumbor stopped and called out, "Hail, guardian. Let me pass. The sun is nearly here!"

Red eyes glared unblinkingly. Boiling water frothed wildly at their feet.

"Come, speak to me," said Thumbor. "I know your power. I have no wish to anger you. My slaves and I must soon be under the hills."

A voice like wood being sawed rasped against their ears, "Come closer." They did.

Thumbor said in a gruff voice, "Keep walking, slaves, while I speak with the master of these mountains." They were beneath threatening branches now. Stiffly Meerlyn and Joel continued walking toward the top of the pass. Thumbor stopped.

The tree's voice again spoke, "Why come you this way, troll?"

Thumbor paused, lowered his voice, "I journey on a secret mission for my master, Dragonel."

The tree said, "So I had supposed. But you act strangely, troll. You have not offered to pay your toll."

Thumbor thought swiftly. He must guess what it was

*The air was filled with knives.*

the tree wanted. He said, "But I must hurry. My master will settle all accounts later."

The tree's voice was as cold as ancient snow, "Your master is not my master. I will live long after he is gone. I have no masters. I am power here."

"Surely!" Thumbor said. "Surely."

He paused, "However, I don't have your payment. Dragonel is sending it later with goblins to guard it."

The tree said, "I drink blood, troll . Blood is my price. If you anger me, I will drink yours. Give me a slave. Now."

Thumbor said, "Of course, of course. I didn't think that you would want such a skinny one. My master will be sending a fatter one along later. But you can have them both."

He stepped out from under the tree and called to Joel, "Slave, stop!"

He turned to the tree and said, "Good, this one often doesn't obey. He is so stupid that the spells put upon him sometimes don't work."

Joel guessed what Thumbor wanted him to do. The big man yelled, "Slave, come here! Slave, come here!" Joel didn't move. "Slave, come here, now!" Joel didn't move. Thumbor cursed and growled, "I'll have to fetch him for you." The tree's limbs stirred restlessly.

Meerlyn was already safely below the top of the pass. Joel was still five yards from the summit. He waited as Thumbor, cursing all the way, walked slowly up to get him. Red eyes bored into his back. His muscles were tensed. He knew that the next moment would bring danger. The next moment came.

Thumbor, close now, whirled and flung his axe. He then threw himself to his left. As he fell he screamed, "Down, Joel, down!" Joel took two steps forward and dove to the ground. The air was filled with knives. Joel felt one pierce his back. Pain burned through him. He thought that he must die from it. A cry exploded from his lips, but it was drowned by a wailing sound from behind him.

Thumbor's axe had bitten deeply into the face of the tree. In a voice of tearing saws it howled its anger and its pain. Its branches beat wildly at the axe, but the bitter axe stayed buried in its wood-flesh. The stricken tree twisted and twisted in the stony ground.

Joel felt Thumbor lift him. Then pain-fire pushed him into darkness.

# XV

## The Healing

Thumbor carried Joel beneath the shade of some young trees. He gently laid his burden on soft, good-smelling pine needles. They had traveled less than a mile from the scene of their battle.

Meerlyn stepped lightly into the grove. She said, "Bramble is keeping watch. How is Joel?"

Thumbor looked up, "He's going to die if we can't help him. His wound is bad enough, but the poison will kill him. He has no more than a few minutes."

Meerlyn knelt beside Joel. She looked at his flushed face. She looked into Thumbor's eyes. "I must use the jewel."

Thumbor said, "My lady!"

"I know." Meerlyn looked down, " But it is the only thing that will help him. I must try."

"My lady," said Thumbor, "the danger is great. Lor's magic is not yours. It has terrible power and the power is not tame."

Meerlyn smiled, "Thumbor, you forget who I am. I know these things. It was once thought in the City of Marl that Lor would come to me. I will not be using the power for myself. That fact will be my robe of safety." Carefully, she opened Joel's shirt.

Thumbor watched. "Touch the jewel only when it is touching, Joel," he advised.

She slowly untied the pouch. Never did she touch Lor. Holding it through the leather she placed it over the boy's heart. She put the pouch by her side. She folded her hands in her lap and sat silently for several moments. At last, she was ready. Softly she said,

In seas of fear
With darkness near
Your strength is sand
Only courage stands
And one thing more—
A star's bright heart—Lor

She reached out and placed both hands on the jewel. Blinding light flashed through the grove. Thumbor cried out. Meerlyn pressed her hands against the jewel. Her face was bright and firm in its fire. Slowly the fire became a glow.

Meerlyn closed her eyes. She was walking across a dark field. Yellow light came from the jewel in her hands. Dry grass turned to gold in its light. Ahead, she saw Joel. He was walking slowly down a hill into great darkness.

She went faster. She didn't call out. She knew that he wouldn't listen. She had to get between him and the darkness. It was very close now. She ran.

She caught him at the utter edge. She stood facing him with her back to misty deeps. She pushed fear from her heart. She placed Lor in Joel's hands. She held his face in her hands and forced him to look into her eyes. Slowly, his mind came back to him.

They stood for long moments looking into each other's eyes. In his deepest dreams Joel would always remember her warm, brown eyes. At last, the poison was beaten.

Meerlyn opened her eyes. Joel was breathing quietly, sleeping. "It is done. He is safe." She carefully wrapped the jewel. She stood. Weakness came over her and she began to fall. Thumbor caught her and helped her to the ground. She did not try to move for many minutes. Finally, her strength began to return.

Thumbor said nothing to her. He could only smile. Sunlight flooded the grove. Pine-scent spiced the last cool airs of morning. Peace was an unbroken circle around

*He was walking slowly down a hill into great darkness.*

them. Then, like a red shadow, Bramble slipped silently into view.

"Friends, goblins come. We must leave here. Now."

Thumbor said, "My Lady, are you well enough?"

She said, "The goblins care not how well I am. I'm as well as I must be." She stood.

Bramble looked at Thumbor, "Which way?"

Thumbor stooped and gently lifted Joel. "Through this grove and on to our left. We have a mile more to go. There will be a stream, and above, it, a cave. We will be safe when we reach that cave."

They were splashing through the stream when the goblins saw them. They heard shrill cries and saw iron swords glint in the sun. Up a slope they ran as the noises behind them grew louder. Behind a boulder they found the cave's dark opening.

"In here," Thumbor shouted.

They rushed through the entrance. With sun-dazzled eyes they ran on into blackness. Torches suddenly flared. Thumbor cried out. He fell forward and Joel slipped from his arms. Nets covered the big man in silver webs.

Bramble barked out, "Ambush!" then dodged as furry paws reached at him from the darkness. His teeth shone in the flickering light. Meerlyn leaped across the fallen Thumbor and knelt beside Joel. She pulled his sword from its scabbard. She raised it high in the air, ready to strike.

A powerful voice shouted, "Stop!" Everyone did. Bramble, teeth bared and back to a corner, looked quickly from side to side. Meerlyn held the sword before her.

A long, glistening shape came forward. It was a silver-furred ottter. His eyes were fixed on the sword in Meerlyn's hands. Other shapes, brown and furry, came into the light. Bright eyes surrounded them. The silver otter stopped. "Girl, you hold a sword which I recognize. The Queen of the Rivers and the Rains, my Queen, told me to befriend the person who wields that sword. This I will do." He stepped closer.

"Wait!" Meerlyn's voice was cold. Her eyes were shaded. "I am Meerlyn, Princess of the High City of Marl. Why did you attack my escort and me?"

The otter bowed. "My lady, your forgiveness! Echoes of surface trouble reached us this morning. We made ready to surprise goblins here. Instead of enemies, we have caught friends."

Meerlyn lowered the sword. "Good otter, we need and accept your welcome. Carry the boy carefully. He has suffered great harm."

The silver otter shouted, "Quick, the troll is getting loose. Kill it." Several large otters moved toward Thumbor.

# XVI

## In Rimbell

Meerlyn shouted, "Wait! He is no troll. He is one of our party. His name is Thumbor and he is a stout friend of all free creatures!"

The otters looked doubtfully at the big man. The silver otter said, "Hold! She must speak the truth. It is far past dawn outside. Sunlight would have killed a true troll." The other otters turned away.

Meerlyn smiled. Thumbor rose to his feet and dusted himself off. He grinned sheepishly as Meerlyn came up to him, "I guess I wasn't much help."

Bramble stepped lightly to her side and said, "You at least might have told us that we could expect to meet friendly creatures down here. Those otters would have been in great trouble if I had not held my anger in check."

Meerlyn laughed and said, "Oh fearsome warrior, I'm sure Thumbor was only giving you a chance to exercise your talents. Isn't that right?"

Thumbor laughed, "In truth, my lady, in truth."

Bramble said, "Well, you might stop your hee-hawing long enough to see to our sick one."

Thumbor's eyes clouded as he remembered Joel's tumble. He turned quickly, but Joel was being well cared-for. Six sleek otters had put him on a low-wheeled cart. They had covered him with warm furs and were waiting patiently for instructions. The silver otter was again beside them.

"Come," said Meerlyn, "our new friends await us."

They walked over to the cart. The silver otter said, "My name is Windrush. I am the leader of my people. Tell me what you need. You will have all of the help that we can give."

Thumbor said, "Windrush, we must travel far and secretively. You know from where we have come. Know also that the Witch Queen seeks us. I have heard that rivers flow beneath mountains and plains. I have heard that your people, the otter tribe, sail these rivers freely. Have I heard truth?"

Windrush said, "You have. To where would you journey?"

Thumbor said, "There is a place, The Plains of Morning, where friends may be waiting for us. Can you take us there?"

The old otter seemed to smile. "I can, and gladly so. First, let us see to your friend. Later, we can feast. While you tell me your tale, the rafts can be prepared. Come, Rimbell, our home, is not grand, but it is a happy place for those who come to it in peace."

Behind them some of the otters were pulling on a chain attached to a large boulder. The boulder was moving inch by inch across the entrance to the cave.

Suddenly, the otters dropped the chain and fell back with shouts of anger and calls for help. A dark, squat figure pushed through the narrow space between the boulder and the cave wall. It was the goblin captain. He brandished his crooked sword and shouted, "Ha, you river-snakes, I've caught you this time! Stand and fight!"

Windrush glanced quickly around the cavern. His otters were not ready to fight off the goblin attack. It would be some minutes before they could arm themselves and assemble. Something had to be done. The goblins could not be allowed to reach the tunnels leading down to Rimbell.

Windrush said, "Ah, captain, you offer me sport. We've long had our differences, you and I. Let us settle them now. Are you brave enough to fight me alone?" He looked at the goblin soldiers crowding in behind their captain. "I wonder?"

The goblin captain spluttered and choked in rage. He flung down his sword and pulled out an evil-looking, black-bladed knife. Finally, he hissed, "Close with me if you dare, otter."

Thumbor, Meerlyn, and Bramble stood close to Joel, ready to defend him from a goblin rush. Otters began to gather silently to either side of them. Windrush smiled, "In the sand pit, captain. Let only the winner come out alive."

A circular pit of silver sand lay below and to one side of the entrance. Its walls were as high as a tall man's shoulders. It was no more than five of Thumbor's steps wide. The goblin captain ran forward, leaped, and landed exactly in the center of the pit. His face was wrinkled in a snarl and his feet were braced wide. Windrush smiled again and glided toward the pit. In one flowing motion he went over its side and down onto the sand.

The goblin rushed forward and aimed a cruel, low slash at the otter's side. Windrush curled around the knife point as it grazed his fur. He then bit deeply into the goblin's exposed arm. The goblin fell back cursing.

Shouts came from the watching goblins. The otters looked on in silence. Bramble licked his lips. Thumbor clinched his fists and wished mightily he had been able to retrieve his axe. Meerlyn knelt beside Joel and kept watch over his restless sleep.

Windrush and the goblin captain circled each other warily. Their eyes shone fiery red in the torchlight. Suddenly, the goblin again charged. He raised his dark knife high above his head. Windrush rose to meet the blow. The knife flashed down. Windrush again ducked under the point of the blade and gripped the goblin's hairy arm in his strong jaws. The goblin howled and the knife flew free of his pain-numbed fingers.

Windrush held on an instant too long. The goblin wrapped his good arm around the otter and squeezed with bone-cracking force. Windrush lunged upward desperately, his jaws seeking the goblin's throat.

Bramble growled softly. Thumbor said, "Easy, Bramble. We can do nothing now."

The otter and the goblin fell, locked together, to the floor of the pit. They rolled over and over scattering a silvery fountain of sand. They rolled to the rock wall and stopped. A long, strangled wail echoed through the cavern. Then—there was silence.

Slowly, slowly Windrush pulled himself over the edge of the pit. The goblin captain lay dead on the sand below him.

The goblin soldiers roared their fury and began to move forward. The otters raised their short swords and round shields. Thumbor braced himself against a boulder and Bramble bared his teeth in a snarl. At that moment, a vast, inhuman cry sounded from the depths of the otter's tunnel. It filled the air with fearful sound and shook the very roots of the mountain.

The goblins stopped, frozen suddenly in place by fear. The cry wavered into silence. Their captain forgotten, the goblins turned and ran toward the narrow entrance. They bit and clawed each other in their frantic haste to get away.

Bramble looked wonderingly at Thumbor. Thumbor released the breath he'd been holding and shrugged his shoulders. All around them otters were smiling and lowering their weapons. Several ran to the chain attached to the great boulder. Again they pulled on it, and with a low rumble the boulder slid against the entrance wall. The cavern was at last sealed.

Windrush, walking stiffly, came up to them and said, "That was stupid of me. I should have known that the goblins would be right on your heels."

Bramble said, "Windrush, you fought wonderfully well. That goblin captain was strong, stronger than anyone I ever hope to meet in battle. But . . ."

Thumbor broke in, "But what was that sound that set the rest of the goblins to running?"

Windrush smiled broadly, "That, my friends, is a great secret of my tribe. You may be the first to have actually seen it work. Come, I'll show it to you."

They walked over to the entrance of a large tunnel. There they found a kind of bellows attached to an intricately carved wooden box. Bramble raised an eyebrow and said, "This is what put those goblins to flight?"

Windrush laughed and said, "In the deepest, darkest rivers live great serpents. They are the most powerful creatures in the world, and are fierce and cunning past imagining. The sound which came from this box is like the battle-cry of one of these serpents. The goblins know it well and fear it beyond death. It surprises me only that they did not run faster than they did."

Bramble said, "Is it—ah—possible that we will meet one of these serpents on our river journey?"

Windrush laughed again and said, "It is possible, but not likely. Only hunger brings them out of their holes. You, Bramble, would not make even a mouthful for one of their kind."

Meerlyn came up to them and said, "Windrush, Joel needs warmth and quiet. We should get him to your city as soon as possible."

Windrush nodded, "Your pardon, Lady. We shall leave at once. It is a journey of some hours, but the way is not difficult."

Meerlyn turned and checked to see if Joel was well secured to the low cart on which he still lay. Thumbor made sure that the fur blankets were in place around him. Windrush and Bramble walked to the front of the cart where several otters awaited them. Windrush nodded and the otters slipped into a harness of finely woven rope. Two places in the harness were empty. Windrush turned to Bramble and said, "Are you up to a bit of exercise, Bramble?"

"Indeed, yes, Windrush. Your tunnels and caverns are safe, but most chilly."

The silver otter and the fox both wriggled into the harness. This was the signal for the beginning of the journey. The cart at once began to move. Meerlyn and Thumbor walked to either side of it. Ahead and behind walked several dozen otter soldiers. An equal number of otters, the regular entrance guard, remained in the cavern.

They walked on smooth, sloping granite. The passage was wide around them. Light from the few torches that they carried was quickly swallowed by the thick darkness. The cold, uncaring weight of the mountain seemed to press down upon them. Time slowed. The journey seemed never-ending.

Then, unexpectedly, the passage widened further. Bright light, sunlight, dazzled their eyes. They stepped out from under a rocky arch and beheld Rimbell, the city of the otters.

Meerlyn said, "Windrush, you said that your city was not grand. But this is the grandest, the most beautiful place I've ever seen!"

Windrush smiled and said nothing. They stood on the edge of a valley. At their feet lay a vast lake. Its clean sun-bright waters entirely filled the bottom of the valley. The sides of the valley were sheer granite cliffs. In several places rivers flowing over the cliffs fell free in shimmering waterfalls for thousands of feet. Nearby, in a sheer rock wall, were the caves and towers of Rimbell.

Thumbor said, "Your home is safe, Windrush. No one could possibly attack you here."

"Yes," said Windrush, "it is safe and we have come to love its beauty well. We cannot grow our own food, but the lake gives us fish and the mountains give us precious stones. This is why we have come to be a trading, far-traveling people."

Bramble chuckled, "You sound as if you would move elsewhere if you could. I think, though, that you would get some loud arguments from those youngsters over there if you ever mentioned that you'd had such a thought." Bramble nodded toward some young otters who were playing noisily not far away. They were fearlessly climbing up a great cliff. One of them at last reached a ledge some hundreds of feet above the water. After a moment's pause, the otter jumped headfirst onto a slick stone slide and came rocketing down to land with a huge splash far out in the lake.

Windrush smiled, "You are undoubtedly right. This is a good home. But," he looked at Meerlyn, "my people would suffer greatly if the lands around us were overrun with goblins."

Meerlyn looked out over the calm lake and said softly, "That will not happen while I live and can fight." There was silence for a moment. A breeze brushed by them.

Thumbor grunted and said, "Which reminds me, Windrush, just how are we to leave this mountain castle of yours?"

Windrush said, "The lake is drained by an underground river. This river is our main trade route, our road to the world outside. Later we will take you to the cavern of leave-taking. Now, though, you need food and rest. Your friend, here, needs to be seen by our healers." He looked down at the sleeping Joel. "Come, the caves of my people are warm and full of light."

They managed to turn the cart onto a narrow ledge. They walked along this ledge for some distance with the lake on one side and a cliff on the other. They reached a tall crack in the rock and went through it. They found themselves in a wide cavern which smelled strongly of fresh-baked bread. Many bright and smiling eyes welcomed them.

# XVII

## Dark River

Hours later they prepared for their departure. They had eaten and slept and eaten again. Stories had been told and songs had been sung. Now, they stood in a cavern near the heart of the mountain.

Deep water flowed slowly by them. Yellow light of lanterns was caught and thrown back by crystals far overhead. Two large rafts loaded with supplies and equipment were tied to the bank. Joel was already sleeping peacefully on the second raft.

Windrush spoke, "May we meet again in happier times. Farewell!"

Meerlyn said, "I will, if fortune grants, visit your country again. You have been kind to strangers and for that you are twice blessed. Good-bye, Windrush, good-bye."

Thumbor said, "Our way still has dangers, but you have lessened them greatly." He patted the heavy short-axe which the otters had given him to replace the one he had lost in the battle with the monster tree. "You have my thanks!"

Bramble simply said, "Farewell."

They boarded the rafts. Thumbor and Bramble took the lead raft. Meerlyn boarded the one on which Joel slept. They all turned and waved. Glider and Goldfur, the two otter crewmen, threw off mooring ropes. The long journey had begun.

For two days Joel did little but sleep. Sleep was his medicine, his nurse. Meerlyn discovered, to her delight, the secret of the tow-fish. For hours she watched them do their work. They never seemed to tire. They were strange creatures; their backs were covered with dim red and green lights. The otters taught Bramble and Thumbor a game played with bones and pearls. Bramble did well at it, but Thumbor always seemed to lose. On such occasions, he was likely to get moody and stare at the water, or whet his new axe-blade.

On the third day Joel awoke and his eyes were bright. He was, understandably, thirsty and hungry. He was also curious. Meerlyn told him all that had happened while he had been sick. He tired soon, though, and slept again for the rest of that day and on through that night.

On the fourth day he awoke and was quiet. It was very strange for him. There had been no change in the darkness. He couldn't tell the length of his wakings and his sleepings. Deep, deep quiet surrounded him. It seemed as if he had been dreaming. It seemed as if all the things that had happened to him were only dreams. He felt a weight on his chest. It was Lor. He untied the pouch and took out the jewel. It glowed softly in the darkness.

Meerlyn sat down beside him. He looked up. Her eyes were looking into his. He said, "You...you saved me. I was dying."

Meerlyn smiled to herself and looked away into the mountain's night, "I only came to find you. Lor saved us."

Joel said, "Still, you came. You hardly know me."

Meerlyn's eyes met his. She said, "You came past the silver snake to find me. You had never even seen me before."

Joel said, "I . . . I didn't know what I was doing. All those things—just happened to me. Following Thumbor finally led me to finding you."

Meerlyn nodded, "Sometimes, that's the way of it."

Joel went on, "I want to thank you. . . ."

"I know that." Meerlyn looked away again. "You don't need to say anything. We're friends and friends give each other help and thanks always, silently. Words often just get in the way."

Joel said, "Yes. I understand that now. There's something else."

Meerlyn looked at him, "What?"

124

Joel paused. He couldn't get what he wanted to say quite straight in his mind. He went ahead anyway, "Telmeer told me some things a long time ago. I didn't understand him. He talked about how I needed help. He said that I should try to help other people. He said that that would make me feel better. I still don't understand what he was trying to tell me. Only—"

Meerlyn was still looking into his eyes. She said nothing.

"Only, I don't feel alone any more. I don't feel alone. I did before. I always did and I never knew it until just before that tree got me." He looked down into the water. Meerlyn still said nothing. She smiled and went to get cakes made of pine-nuts and honey.

Later, they all sat together on a sandy beach far underground. The river flowed quietly past them. Light from their oil lamps flickered on the water and glinted from half-hidden crystals in the walls. Glider and Goldfur were off searching for crayfish, a great delicacy to them.

Bramble said, "I can eat fish, but I greatly prefer rabbit."

Thumbor chuckled, "I will personally catch one for you when we reach the Plains of Morning."

Meerlyn said, "Will that be soon?"

Thumbor pursed his lips, "I believe so. Being underground has confused me greatly, but I think we have come nearly halfway."

Joel said, "Can we really expect help there?"

Thumbor smiled, "It is certain. I'm sure that the King will be waiting with a force of men. He has probably been there since before we met, Joel. Telmeer and I agreed that that would be a good ending place for this adventure."

Meerlyn said, "My father will be there."

They were silent for awhile. Darkness was soft around them. Thumbor broke the silence at last, "Bramble, once you said you would give us the story of your quest. Why not now?"

Bramble grinned, "Ah, my friends. Later. Later. I am in no mood for tale-telling."

Joel said, "Bramble, do tell us something. Please."

"Alright," the fox laughed, "but only a short version. I have spirit for no more than that. "Well," he paused, "In faraway Kor-Narl there is a treasure of great beauty and . . ."

Suddenly, a whirling glow of colored light filled the cavern. The four friends leaped to their feet, Bramble's story forgotten. They rushed to the water's edge and looked down. They beheld a wonder.

Thousands upon thousands of fish were swimming just below the surface. Their bodies shone with light. They circled twice around the wide expanse of the cavern.

Bramble saw it first and barked with surprise. Each of the others gasped in turn. A serpent, twice as long as one of their rafts, slowly rose out of darkness. Its body was covered with scales of midnight blue. Its mouth was full of needle-teeth. Its eyes glowed golden in the light from the terrified school of fish.

In a heartbeat it was among the fish. Its four stubby fins had scarcely moved. With two quick gulps it swallowed hundreds of fish.

Its meal completed, the serpent rose to the surface. As its head broke into the air, it opened its mouth. A vast, lonely cry—the same cry which had so frightened the goblins in the entrance cave—echoed through the cavern.

Then, slowly, lazily, it swam close to the watchers on shore. One great eye looked at them with mild interest. Joel shivered, but the serpent moved away from them. Quickly, it faded back into the deep heart of the river. It was gone.

The four friends looked at each other. They found that they had been joined by the two otters. One of them, Glider, said, "Usually they don't come up from their deep places. This one did. We had better leave."

No one disagreed.

# XVIII

## Last Battle

Joel and Meerlyn talked a great deal in the long days of their journey. They shared funny stories and all the odd facts which travelers collect. They even played the game of bones and pearls together. The otters gladly taught it to them. Those were full hours, happy times.

On the tenth day the journey ended and there was sadness in that ending. The two rafts had held them together, safe from danger, and had helped their happiness grow. They waved to Glider and Goldfur and watched the rafts disappear. Stillness surrounded them. They drew out the point of ending. They all knew that they might never again be together as they had been on the journey just ended. They could only hope that the future would hold more times of friendship. They turned and began the long uphill walk which would bring them again into the open air.

They soon found themselves standing among dark oaks. A doorway opened into the hill behind them. Ahead was a rock-filled gully. Dense brush and trees rose on either side of the gully.

Thumbor said, "That is our way." He pointed down the gully. "It should lead us to the Plains of Morning. We'll camp there tonight. Friends should be near. We can find them in the morning."

Bramble said, "More walking? My paws have gotten too soft for this!"

Meerlyn laughed, "It's only a small way, Bramble. We will have safe sleeping in the open. Also, I know of a spring which has cold, cold water. It will make your paws feel wonderful."

Joel was not happy about the decision to walk more. He was still very stiff and very weak. But he followed without complaining as the others set off down the dry stream-bed.

They walked for several minutes. The walls of the little canyon rose steeply around them. Joel began to feel uneasy.

He heard a noise above and behind him. He started to turn, but at that moment something hit him in the back. A heavy weight was carrying him to the ground. Gray shapes were leaping through the air all around him. Wolves. He smashed into the ground and fought to keep conscious. His companions struggled in the ambush.

A wolf grazed past Meerlyn's shoulder. She dodged to the side of the gully. She still wore Joel's sword. With a rock wall at her back she drew it and began to fight.

Bramble also sought safety for his back. He made a twisting turn which caused a wolf's teeth to close on air instead of on his back. His return bite opened the side of his attacker's face. The wolf jumped back.

Thumbor threw a wolf off of his back. The creature tumbled through the air like a falling kite. It landed hard and did not move. Thumbor raised his new axe and began to fight. With each terrible stroke a wolf died.

Meerlyn faced three snarling faces. She could not leave herself open for long enough to get in a telling blow. None of the wolves, however, dared come within the shining circle she made with Joel's sword.

Bramble still fronted the beast whose face he had gashed. The shaggy shoulders and head raised into the air as if the creature was going to jump high and come down in a crushing attack. This was an old fighting trick of the wolf tribe. It worked. Bramble braced himself and raised his head to meet the high attack. The wolf dove low. Bramble's right leg snapped in its strong jaws. It dodged back.

Joel raised himself from the ground. The wind had been knocked out of him. His shoulder hurt terribly where his wound had been. The wolf had knocked him down and left him. It had gone on to fight Bramble. Joel stood up. Then, he saw Bramble.

The fox was standing on three legs. The wolf was closing in. Bramble was preparing to sell his life dearly. Joel stooped and picked up a large rock. Pain stabbed along his left arm and through his back. He staggered forward with the rock raised high. The wolf leaped. Joel cast the rock. It struck the beast's side, knocking it to the ground.

It got up slowly and limped away. Joel and Bramble turned to find Meerlyn and Thumbor now standing together facing a snarling half-circle of wolves. Five of the beasts leapt toward them at the same time. One lost its head to the mighty downstroke of Thumbor's axe and another was killed by the return stroke. One was plucked out of the air by the big man's strong left hand and thrown shatteringly to the ground. Another was knocked spinning by his heavy boot. The last wolf ran itself heart-deep on Joel's sword which Meerlyn held with both hands. Those wolves that remained stood silently, watching, tongues lolling, yellow-eyed with hatred and fear. Then they faded like gray shadows into the rocks and were gone.

Suddenly, the friends were alone. They began to smile at each other. Their smiles quickly died as a low, wild moaning—the sound of northern winds captured and braided with ropes of darkness—curled from dusky shadows. A circle of light, pale as the bellies of dead fish, formed in the air above a squarish boulder. Cold dread filled the hearts of the watching friends. The circle of light grew brighter and a figure appeared in its center. The Witch Queen had come.

She was clothed in gray and upon her head rested an iron crown. Her left hand was hidden in mist. Her right hand held a spear longer than a man is tall. Her face was white and scarred like storm-torn mountain stone. Her eyes were as red as flaming blood. She stared at them, her bristling brows a straight line.

The friends looked down. They could not bear the gaze of those terrible eyes. The Witch Queen laughed and her steely teeth glinted. She laughed and the sound of her laughter was as soft as rolling waves of black velvet.

At last, she said, "I have come for you, Meerlyn. My business with you is not yet done. These others," she glanced at the fox, the boy, and the man, "have caused me much trouble. They will die, but slowly. Now . . ." The mist around the Witch's left hand began to grow.

Thumbor chose that moment to throw his axe. It flew straight toward the Witch Queen. She didn't try to dodge it. It struck her, passed into her, and disappeared. The big man shouted, "Joel, use Lor! It's a sending. Her body isn't here. Use Lor!"

Joel reached for the jewel. It was warm against his chest even through its leather pouch. The Witch Queen smiled again. The smile was as cold as a shark's eye. She raised the red spear. Joel saw that it was pointed right at him. He had no time to be afraid. He fumbled with the leather thongs Thumbor had made.

The Witch's eyes blazed. She threw the spear. Like a snake's darting tongue it flew. Joel raised his arm. Suddenly, a shadow fell across him. It was Thumbor. Thumbor had jumped between him and the Witch.

The big man tried to hit the darting spear with his hand. Only his fingers moved. He had no time. The spear went deep into his chest. He fell.

Too late. Too late. Too late, Joel began shouting the words of the old verse,

*"In seas of fear . . ."*

Too late, Lor was burning fiercely in his hand,

*"With darkness near . . . "*

Too late, the Witch Queen screamed her anger and her pain.  Joel's voice was steady,

*"Your strength is sand . . . "*

The jewel's white light was crumbling her into mist,

*"Only courage stands . . ."*

The wild face became swirls of grayness,

*"And one thing more . . . "*

Lor burned,

*"A star's bright heart—Lor".*

Joel ran to Thumbor.  Meerlyn was already kneeling by his side.  The spear had vanished along with the Witch Queen.  The wound had not.  Bright blood welled from it. The big man could not speak.  He could only try to breathe. He finally took a deep breath and held it.  He lifted his hand.  Joel took it.  Thumbor looked deep into the boy's eyes and smiled.  Then, he died.

# XIX

## Partings

Bramble could not walk. He stayed beside Thumbor's body. He could forget the pain from his torn leg because the pain in his heart was greater. Meerlyn and Joel searched through the forest for broken branches. They could not bury their friend. They had to make him a pyre. They would give his ashes to the winds.

They gathered wood until nearly dawn. Meerlyn knew something about this kind of funeral. She placed the wood around Thumbor's body and at his feet she positioned one of the dead wolves.

At last, the sad work was done. Joel took a burning branch from the small fire they had made earlier. He held it in his hand. For long minutes he looked at Thumbor's still face. Then, with the rising of the sun, he thrust his brand in among dry sticks. They all watched as flames were born and began to grow. When only ashes remained, they turned and left that place forever.

Meerlyn carried Bramble in her arms. She tried to be gentle. The fox was in great pain. Joel walked stiffly behind her. They said nothing at all.

The Plains of Morning were wide and calm. Young grass and sunlight were everywhere. Close by there was the sound of water falling over small stones. At the small stream they stopped to drink and rest. Telmeer found them there.

The old man was riding a gray horse. With him were eleven mounted men. Meerlyn looked up. Joy filled her heart. Carefully, she placed Bramble in Joel's arms. She turned and ran. A stout, bearded man leaped down from his horse and ran to meet her. It was the King. They both stopped when they were within a few feet of each other.

For a moment they looked into each other's eyes. Then, they embraced.

Telmeer dismounted and walked up to Joel. The boy's eyes were dull with tiredness and hurting. Telmeer saw this. He saw how thin the boy's body had become. He saw the wounded fox lying quietly in Joel's arms. He saw that Thumbor was not there. With no words spoken he knew much of what had happened. He put his hand gently on Joel's shoulder.

The King's men made camp among trees on the edge of the open spaces. Yellow tents were raised and the horses were freed to feast on meadow grass. Telmeer took care of Bramble. Joel sat on short grass near a patch of orange wildflowers. His mind was numb with pain and grief. Morning sun warmed him. Soon, he slept.

Some hours later, he was awakened by the sound of a soft voice. Telmeer was talking to him, "Joel, Joel, Bramble wants to see you."

Joel sat up. He felt confused, empty. He managed to say, "Bramble? Where? How . . . how is he?"

Telmeer said, "He's badly hurt, but he should live. He will have the best of care. Come, he's over in the yellow tent."

Joel rose and followed Telmeer. They reached the tent. Joel went in. Telmeer waited outside.

Bramble was lying on a large hammock. Beneath and around him was a soft blanket. He looked terribly small and lifeless against its whiteness. For a moment, fear stabbed through Joel's heart. Then Bramble lifted his head.

"Joel, they've got me wrapped up like a Christmas pie. I can hardly move!"

Joel smiled wanly, "Well, stay still then. You wouldn't want to spoil Telmeer's fox pie, would you?" It was a terrible joke and Joel knew it.

*Bramble was lying on a large hammock.*

There was a long, awkward pause. He looked at the floor. There was only coldness, emptiness inside of him. Thumbor was dead. Thumbor was dead. He could hide nowhere from that truth. He slumped to his knees. He shook his head, "Bramble, why did it happen? Why, Bramble, why?"

The fox looked out of the tent's open doorflap. Breeze stirred leaves on an oak nearby. Bramble said, "I can't give you any answer. Snows fall. Streams flow. Friends die."

Joel pounded his fist on the dirt, "It's not fair! He shouldn't have had to die! It's not fair!"

"Joel," Bramble's voice was soft. "Joel," the boy raised his eyes. "Be sad. That is a good, a true feeling. You've earned that feeling with your love. Don't feel cheated, or bitter as you once did. We all must die. You, too, some-day. The way you die has much to do with the way you've lived. Thumbor knew this. He loved you well and he died saving you. His was a hard death, but he would have chosen no other."

Joel said nothing. He slowly reached out and stroked the soft fur of Bramble's back. He had not dared to do this since the day that they first met in the pit of spears. The fox closed his eyes. They were both quiet for a time. Joel's mind emptied of all thoughts. He felt only the soft-ness of Bramble's fur. He knew for a few moments the peace of forgetfulness.

Then Bramble opened his eyes. He blinked and said, "Well, they'll be taking me away tonight. Telmeer says I may lose my leg." He looked down at his bandages. "But he wants some friend of his—Pollywall, Pollywumpus, or some such thing—to look at it before they carve. I will be laid up for some time, I fear."

Joel said, "Bramble, I'll come with you."

"No," the fox said quietly, "I must take my medicine, whatever it is, alone. You still have Lor, Joel. You may be needed again. Stick with Telmeer. Stay close to the old man."

Joel looked down.

Bramble chuckled, "Never fear, Joel Burnham, we'll be together again. I can see that I'll have years more of being your nursemaid. You are a very clumsy boy. Besides, I still haven't told you the tale I promised."

Joel smiled. He said, "Bramble, I'll come to you as soon as I can. I promise." The fox nuzzled his hand and smiled in return. Joel rose to his feet. Bramble weakly lowered his head. Joel left his friend's side. He stopped as he reached the tent's doorflap and looked back. Bramble was asleep. Sadness burned in his eyes like driven snow. He stumbled outside.

Meerlyn was waiting for him. She said, "Joel, my father and I are needed back in Marl. There is much there that needs doing. For part of the way we will be riding with Bramble. I'll take care of him."

Joel looked at the ground and said nothing. He knew he should speak, but words wouldn't come.

Meerlyn went on, "Telmeer told me that he wants you to travel to the East with him. That's a good idea. I hope that you do. I also hope that you will visit me in Marl when your journeys are done."

Joel looked up, "I will, Meerlyn. I want to see your city. Only now. . . too much has happened. I need to think."

Meerlyn reached out and took his hand, held it tightly, "Joel, I know. I know. You came far and suffered much on my account. I will never forget all that you've done. The closest place to my hearthfire will always be yours." She released his hand. "Now, I must prepare for tonight's leave-taking. Good-bye . . . and good fortune wherever you fare."

Joel smiled and said, "Good-bye, Meerlyn, good-bye."

Meerlyn's eyes were bright with tears. She turned and walked back to her father's pavillion. Joel wandered down to the small stream. Telmeer found him there.

"Joel, I'm leaving here. There is still danger in this land. I want to watch and listen for awhile. Will you come with me?"

Joel didn't care where he was. But to move, to walk would be better than to sit in one place. He said, "Yes, I'll go with you, Telmeer."

They walked away from the camp that very hour. They left quietly with quiet farewells. There would be another time for great speeches and celebrations.

Just as they passed the last tent, they were hailed from behind. They both turned. A man dressed in hunting leathers and a rough green cloak came walking swiftly up to them. Telmeer went down on one knee. Joel looked at the old man in surprise and then back at the newcomer. Embarrassment suddenly flooded through him, and he, too, knelt before Morgan Balfour, Meerlyn's father, King of Tananar.

The King said, "Rise, my friends. This is not court. There is no need for formality here."

Joel rose and looked curiously at the King. His glance took in a sturdy, wide-bodied, thick-armed man who from behind could easily be mistaken for a farmer or a blacksmith. But Morgan's eyes gave the lie to any such notions. They were the eyes of a king—deep, wise and calm.

The King continued, "I thought that you were both asleep still. I had planned to honor you tonight at my table. I came quickly when I learned of your departure."

Telmeer said, "Sire, I would have told you of our plans, but you were at council. I thought it best not to disturb you."

"I understand, Telmeer. I also understand the wisdom of your taking leave without fanfare. Still, I wanted to speak with Joel." Morgan's eyes turned toward him. Joel met the King's gaze and found in it warmth and truthfulness. The doors of his pain-barred heart opened wide. Without another word being spoken Joel gave the promise of his lifelong loyalty to the King. It was accepted without words and without words the King promised his friendship in return. Then Morgan smiled and continued, "Joel, I owe you as much as one man can owe another man. You and Thumbor and Bramble saved Meerlyn, my only child, from death. My kingdom, as much of it as you want, is yours."

Joel looked down and said nothing. Embarrassment and not a little anger reddened his face. He did not wish to be rewarded, paid for what he had done.

Morgan's hand gently touched Joel's chin, raised his face. Again, Joel looked into the King's calm eyes. Morgan said, "Do not be offended, Joel. Honor demands that I offer you gifts, just as honor demands that you refuse them. Go now with my blessing and with my friendship . . . wherever you fare." Morgan grasped Joel's shoulders, pulled him close, embraced him. Then, releasing Joel, he took Telmeer's hand and said, "Take care, old friend. And come to me soon!"

Telmeer said, "I will, Sire. Good-bye."

Joel smiled and said, "Good-bye, Sire."

Morgan looked at them both once again with a smile in his eyes and then turned to walk back into camp.

Telmeer took Joel across the Plains of Morning. They were on foot and carried only a small amount of food. They traveled for days, sleeping beneath the stars, seeking out small towns when they needed to buy bread.

Slowly, Joel told the story of his adventures to the old man. Quietly as the coming of a summer evening, gentle sorrow replaced the bitter loss in Joel's heart.

One rainy night, Telmeer and Joel sat huddled close to their fire. Telmeer said, "Joel, soon, I suspect, Lor will take you back to your own world."

Joel looked up, "How do you know that?"

Telmeer smiled, "After all, I am a wizard of sorts. I have a feel for such things."

Joel looked back at the flames. "I don't want to go."

Telmeer sighed, "You won't have much choice. For a time you and Lor won't be needed in Tananar. Evil creatures have drawn back to the West. We have found that out in our wanderings. You greatly hurt the Witch, though she will not die. You knew that, didn't you?"

Joel looked at Telmeer, "I felt that she wasn't dead. Thumbor said that her attack on us was a sending. I suppose that's some sort of magic."

"It is. What you did to her caused her to pull back her forces. She will brood long in her dark tower. Pain will weigh upon her mind. But she will heal. You will be needed again, I'm sure. You and Lor."

Joel said, "'I still don't want to leave."

Telmeer said, "Joel, we can't control that. Your being here creates . . . an imbalance. Lor's power brought you. You really belong in your own world. Only overpowering need can call you here. For now, the danger has passed. Don't worry. Danger will be great again. The Witch Queen will see to that. Your fate is bound up with hers. You will fight her again—and Dragonel, too, I should think. Remember, Rhiannon is still within the walls of Toadhorn. Someday, I will try to free her. I shall want you with me then."

Joel said nothing. For awhile there was only the sound of raindrops on leaves.

Telmeer glanced at the boy, "Are you afraid to go back, afraid of your troubles there?"

Joel raised his eyes, "No. They don't worry me at all." He looked down again into hissing flames. "A long time ago you talked about names, about how no names fit you. Well, back in my world mine no longer fits me. Too much has happened to me here. I'll never again do the mean things, the stupid things I used to do."

"You will be sorely tested."

Joel grinned, "I guess so. It will take time for people to see that I've changed. But they will. I know they will."

"Then—what does bother you about returning?"

"Leaving my friends. I'd be leaving Bramble, Meerlyn —and you."

Telmeer smiled, "Joel, we will be here always and will always be your friends. Trust me. I know that you will make new friends back in your world. And I know that you will someday come back here."

Joel said nothing and stared into the fire. Rain came down harder. They pulled their cloaks tighter and listened to darkness roar around them.

Morning broke into a clearing sky. They traveled on.

Late that afternoon they climbed a low hill. On its other side they found the sea. They stayed on the crown of that hill, resting. The sun fell behind them. Golden light called forth wondrous greens from distant waves. The fresh dampness of a sea breeze cooled them.

Joel watched the sea. He felt sadness leaving him— the sadness of Thumbor's death, the sadness and anger of his father's death. Tears came to his eyes. He cried. He cried and Telmeer held him. The sun fell further and the breeze died.

Sweet calm followed tears. The old man and the boy rose to their feet. They walked down the hill's far side. They walked over sand and came to the sea's edge. Gentle wave-sounds washed around them. They stood there together as stars rose above the Eastern rim of the world. They watched the coming of the stars and were glad.

# The
# End